Tinder Nights With Tracey

Swiping Right During The Age of The Rona

Tracey M. Kennedy

Copyright © 2022 by Tracey M. Kennedy

ISBN: 9798371152077

All rights reserved.

Based upon a true story. Names and events have been altered to protect the identity of individuals involved.

No part of this book may be reproduced, or stored in a retrieval system, or transmitted in any form or by any means, electronic, mechanical, photocopying, recording, or otherwise, without express written permission of the author.

Cover Photography by: Kimber Greenwood

Graphic Design by: Mellonee Mayo

Printed in the United States of America

Contents

Dedication	1
Epigraph	2
Preface	3
1. The Catalyst	5
2. Creating A Roster	19
3. Tryouts	29
4. Switching Out Players	44
5. I Don't Even Like Sports	53
6. The World Stopped	62
7. Like, Like Liquor…	76
8. Now, It's Time for A Breakdown	93
9. Babylon	107
Epilogue	124
About Author	125
Acknowledgments	126

Notes

This is dedicated to me! Just kidding. I dedicate this book to every person I have been in conact with throughout my life. Each soul has shaped and molded me into the woman I am today. Whether you brought joy or heartache to my world, I thank you. I'm whole because of you.

And, to you...You pushed me past my limits. You broke me like an animal. Thank goodness I'm protected by the ancestors, thank goodness I have nine lives, thank goodness you forced me to be a better woman. I have never loved another man more.

He loved when I wore red lipstick. It turned him on the see the color smeared across my complexion as he fucked my head into the pillows from the back. I would talk to him for brief moments before sex as time went on between us. On occasions, it felt like he fucked me with passion when he knew I was feeling sadness and longing for Black King. His stroke would make me forget everything. It was like taking pure uncut ecstasy. It was smooth, and penetrating. Deep and spirit shaking. He treated my pussy like he was applying to get into heaven. Professing how beautiful I was to him, "I love looking into your eyes when I nut. It takes me to another world."

-Frat Boy Slim

Preface

Considering the fact that I'm such a big personality, I do enjoy hiding in the shadows often. With that said, I never had any intentions of writing this book. My life became such a whirlwind of events, I daydreamed daily, working to figure out how to climb out of the mental hole I had fallen into. It was a mental hole I would continue to climb out of and fall back into in the most repetitious manner. My only emotional release was writing.

To escape the dumpster fire that had become my marriage, I scrolled Tinder and started writing what I then posted on social media. My hidden suffering turned into weekly entertainment of dating disappointments, and with each step, learning a little bit more about me.

I don't know where this life is going to take me. I can face the world feeling free at my core now, and for a Black women born and raised in America?

Bitch, I'm rare!

Therefore, ipso facto, plurbis ammunition mutha fucka! I'm not giving you any hints or anything! Nope. Just know, you might need a diaper. You may pee yourself from laughing so hard. I'm so funny guys. WOW! Also, some tissue because there will definitely be some sad moments. Do not have any sharp objections around, while playing John Legend music either!

Not because of me though.

John's music just makes you wanna slit your wrists...It's so overly dramatic and grossly lovesick. Vomit.

Anyhoo- Enjoy the book!

ONE

The Catalyst

As soon as he popped up on my screen, "Chile, they have men that look like this in Birmingham?? Bitch where? Swipe RIGHT!!" Instant match, so that means he saw me first and liked what he saw. I didn't remotely play it cool. Immediately, I sent a bunch of thirsty ass eyeball emojis. Yeah, sweet Daddy, I'm looking at you. He was cool in his response though, "Hello Tracey. How are you doing tonight?" In my mind I said, "I'm going to be doing amazing, if I end up fucking you tonight", but I briefly mentioned my day, and then asked if he wanted to meet for drinks later. His response, exactly something I would say, "I'm intrigued". We exchanged numbers and I called him once I was done for the evening.

Ya know, there wasn't one part of me that ever fathomed I would've been a 38-year-old woman, recently separated from her husband, but still living under the same roof, with two kids, looking for a date on Tinder. "I'm too much for you, and you're not enough for me. I'm finally done. I can't do this anymore with you." That's what I told my then husband, Captain Patriarchy, as I drove my cherry red Kia Rio rental car down the 15 freeway in Southern California, while he sat in our home in Alabama. I couldn't take another day of our relationship consistently being about him.

It was always about his big ass fucking feelings.

California weather is typically always amazing, but that day in May 2019? The sun hit different that day. It felt brighter. I felt brighter. I was like a piece of Ikea furniture. I was building myself, and upon completion, I realized there was an extra screw I didn't really need after all. My husband was that extra screw Ikea gives you. I just didn't fucking need him, but everyone made me feel like I couldn't do life without him. They made me feel like I would never find anyone better than him. Like, he was my savior. Years of him being glorified as my lord to the point he moved himself into the role. My DNA mutated into Zero Fucks Given and I completely finished with being married to the man he became.

When I left Captain Patriarchy, I was coming into my own. I was learning how to stand on my own two feet. I had all this power and strength deeply burning inside my being and I was ready to set everything in my path on fire with each breath I exhaled. I owned myself for the first time in my life. As I typed those words, my lips automatically marched into smile mode. I was ready for the best me and past due for some new dick in my life. I totally winked when I wrote that. Thinking about good dick will always do that to me.

I met a king-size chocolate male model who lived in Chicago when I went to the very first Wakandcon the year prior. "I'm happily married with kids, but I had to let you know, you fine as hell. Sexy ass...When you go home, you better call your mama and daddy and thank them for creating you." I wasn't happily married, but it set my boundaries, and still got his attention. He laughed and came to my booth where I was selling my organic body care line, California Country Organics Body Care. "If you follow me on Instagram, I'll give you a free sample." Chicago Dick pulled out his phone from the back pocket of his black jeans and opened Instagram to follow me. "What do you think I should try?" "Since you have a beard, you should try my Hair Vittles Beard and Scalp Nourishment. You should let me rub it into your beard. Everyone needs a little bit of me on their face." I said it with what was supposed to be an innocent grin. When his stare caught my eyes, that's where Chicago Dick and I became friends.

We chatted from time to time for a few months after we met, but when the creators of Wakandacon started sending out emails announcing the dates for the new year, he and I began speaking more frequently. Our innocent flirting stopped being innocent and next thing you know; we are planning sexual escapades for my hotel room once I was to arrive back in Chicago for the event.

Wakandacon brought about this insatiable desire for Black men inside of me. The event made me feel like a gay club at midnight; it was raining men!! I constantly wanted my body draped in melinated, kinky haired Gods.

That's what Black men have become to me, in a physical sense.

When I left for Wakandacon the end of July, I was fucking Captain Patriarchy almost every day for two months after separating and just before returning to Wakandacon. My middle-aged woman hormones were starting to kick in and feeling free to do whatever I wanted kind of made fucking him seem exciting. "Yeah, girl...this is always going to be my pussy. No matter who we are with, you are always going to be mine." Maybe hearing him stake claim to me in any way brought back the passion we once shared in the beginning of our courtship. Ten years is a long time to walk away from and start over also, ya dig? All that sex, but it was still the same self-serving dick. It was always about his dick. And, it wasn't good enough to keep me in an unhappy marriage. He packed condoms in my luggage and sent me a text after I left saying, "Enjoy yourself." I didn't even think about condoms. He did. He has always been cautious and careful in that regard. It was strange and uncomfortable, but I can assure you I followed through.

Chicago Dick and I made plans to have sex the first night I drove into the city. I had just ended my period and I thought I was good to go. When he arrived to my dingy low budget hotel room, I was so nervous. It had been almost ten years since I had sex with anyone other than my husband. It was supposed to be only my Captain for the rest of my life. What was I doing? What if I am a disappointment to this man? This hotel room looks like they just removed the body of a dead hooker from 1988. This isn't exactly how I pictured this situation before getting here. But, now we are here. My anxiety was through the roof.

Another man was going to touch me. I opened the door.

Another man was going to touch me. He smiled at me with this goofy smile he always gives and walked through the doorway. He took off his shoes, and flopped on the bed next to me where I sat slightly stiff, in a white lace rob. I scooted to the top of the bed to lean against the headboard. He leaned back with me as we spoke about the music we enjoyed to break the ice. I horribly sang Hootie and the Blowfish songs to a man ten years younger than me. He had no clue what I was talking about. He could sense that I didn't know what I was doing, however. He offered to give me a massage and I handed him a jar of muscle rub that I make. I turned over onto my stomach as he helped me take off the robe. Hearing the jar open caused me to jump a bit. It's about to happen. This is how it starts.

I was going to have another man touch me. I started shaking.

I almost put my robe back on to change my decision, then his hands stopped rubbing and I felt his lips kiss down my spine. I pictured his touch being smoother. I envisioned this all around lover, capable of any sexual activity known to man. He will forever be my sweet gentle giant man that bumbled through sensually working to entice me. I took a deep breath in. He pawed at my torso to turn me over and passionately placed his lips against mine. Before we met up I told him I wanted him to fuck me like a love song. He delivered. He moved down my body to spread my legs open. He looked between my legs, smiled and winked at me, then proceeded to clean my labia with his tongue. He sent sensations through my body I had not experienced in years. Captain Patriarchy has never really been good at gobbling pussy. Chicago Dick had my hands grabbing for thin air.

My vagina betrayed me! When he came up for air, blood was dripping from his beard. I pointed out that I was bleeding, but he winked at me again, dove back into my ocean and growled deeply. I could feel the vibration through my entire body. By the time we were finished, there was blood and sweat splattered on the sheets, the blankets, mattress cover, the mattress, the floor, and the wall that he picked me up and fucked me against.

"Hello? May I have new sheets for my room? Excuse me? Are you for real?" I called the front desk and they told me I needed to bring down the old sheets in order to get new ones. I face palmed myself. Rarely am I embarrassed, but this was definitely one of those moments. I had no choice to get new sheets, however. Chicago Dick collected all the

Linen and walked down to the front desk with me to trade sheets and blankets. "You might not want to touch these directly" I told her as she began to grab the fabrics from Chicago Dick.

"What's on them? Do I even want to know?" The employee looks at me, then at Chicago Dick, then he looks at me, I look at him, I look at the clerk, and then she says, "I'm just going to go grab some gloves and a bag." We exchanged sheets. It was weird.

Three of the four nights I was there, Chicago Dick and I had sex. That man fucked me like a Teddy Pendergrass song each time. I had never experienced anything like that. I craved it like raw flesh on a lion's lips.

When I came home, he stopped talking to me as much, and after the dick down he gave me, I had no desire to fuck my husband. When the Captain told me, "I'm sorry I gave you the wrong impression. I will never give you the emotional support you need.", and then turned around two days later and had the sheer audacity to look me in my fucking face and ask, "I was wondering if you could give me some emotional support?" There was no fucking WAY I was going to even allow him to see me naked! FUCK YOU DICKHEAD! I looked him in his fucking face and said, "Go find a new bitch". I decided to sign up for Tinder later that night. The photos and profiles were so funny and strange sometimes; I started screenshotting profiles one night and started a Facebook post called, Tinder Nights with Tracey. Over 600 comments on the first post with less than 200 people that consistently follow my private page, it became a weekly thing I did along with updating who I matched with and whom I actually met. When I swiped right on Black King August 5th, Chicago Dick stopped talking to me completely. I tried to keep things going. I mean, he ate my pussy while I was on my period and growled. Of course, I wanted to stay. He wouldn't respond to me however. It stung. He still follows me on my social media platforms however.

Dripping in Alabama humidity, I had a booth at the first Woodlawn Night Market. It was a huge success! I bought myself a pair of broccoli earrings made out of pearler beads, which were created by Exalting in Beauty. They matched my green eyeshadow, and my afro had me looking like Jet Beauty of the Week August 10th 1975. He waited five days to respond to my thirsty ass eyeball emojis. As soon as he responded, I created an emergency Tinder Nights with Tracey dedicated solely to the night I was about to have with him.

After breaking down my booth, paying taxes to the coordinator, Black King called me as I was sitting in my 2015 grey Honda Odyssey counting the money I made. I sat in my car for about a half hour chatting away with him. He seemed so excited to just speaking. He mentioned his complexion throughout the year, which I could totally relate too because come mid-October, my melanin packs up for the winter and doesn't come back until April at the earliest. "When you're around me, you're always going to have to wear heels. I don't really like short women because I don't like bending down, but I'm making the exception for you. I really want to meet you." This Black King seemed overly excited about being in the presence of me. He told me he wanted to super like me, but I said in my profile that I didn't like thirsty men, so he just swiped right in hopes of. It was arrogant and endearing. In hopes of? He knew I was going to swipe right on his fine ass. He told me he was raised by and prefers tall women. I dramatically white woman fainted in my mind. I would never be tall. I will forever be a tiny, pocket-sized woman with the personality of 50 6'9" men. That's all I bring to the table.

Oh, Dear God. He talked sooooooo much. I made a sad face in my mind. This man is going to get on my nerves if he talks as much as I do. That's why his fine ass is on Tinder. UGH

Also, that may be why my fine ass was on Tinder too...I found my match!

Based upon the phone conversation, we decided to meet at Collins Bar in Downtown Birmingham Alabama for two hours. He had to go back to study for the police academy and I was exhausted from being on my feet for hours in Alabama summer heat. I told him I needed to shower, but he said he didn't mind and he would see me shortly. We were only supposed to have a few drinks then part ways. It was already well past 9pm. I parked a block away and arrived to the bar first. I ordered my drink, waiting for his text to tell me he was there.

Black King texted that he was walking up as I was paying for the gin concoction.

I grabbed my drink and began walking towards the door as I scouted for a free table. Have you ever had one of those moments where you could feel the presence of someone without them being in the room? That's what happened. The closer I approached the door, a feeling of warmth washed through my body. I looked up and there he was. Everything faded away and all I could see was him. It felt like my body housed the souls of one thousand civilizations throughout time ready to bow in the presence of what once was their king. Each step he created shook the world around me with dominance and grace. When his eyes connected with mine, his smile melted every cell in within me.

I had felt that smile and that presence in lifetimes before. I couldn't believe what was taking place. One week prior, I was digging in my garden speaking to the ancestors. I was asking for the man I thought

I wanted. "I want someone, strong, and smooth, and emotionally detached. I want a big dick and a great smile. I want someone goal oriented and not afraid to get everything they want. I want a Black man fully aware and proud of his Blackness..." As I dug in soil I created from compost, I dragged on about this magical man I was conjuring up in my head. I was so very specific in my needs and desires. Here he was. The ancestors challenged me. "Oh you think you're ready for that man? You still aren't admitting some things and you want your King? Ok, Tracey. Since you begging for him..."

I definitely wasn't ready for the man I needed.

The night was amazing. Everything seemed like it was natural. This Black King made me feel...safe. I had never felt safe in that capacity with any man, let alone a "stranger". He wasn't a stranger to my spirit however. He was my missing piece. When I leaned in to kiss him, I...I just...It was over three years ago and I still get a bit teary eyed thinking about his lips against mine. Time stopped. When I pulled back from his face, his eyes were still closed. He felt it too. I know he did. As his eyes opened, a smile grew upon his face.

This Black King of mine; didn't smell like any man I have been around in my entire life. When my therapist asked what he smelled like, all I replied with was a blank stare and, "Mercy and grace." I couldn't explain what this man was making me feel. It was something so new and unexpected. Every time I breathed him in, I received an unworldly surge through my veins. I took off my shoe and gently nudged his leg. There was an insignificant man working to waste the precious time I had with my Black King. He saw me earlier at the market and decided to take another chance at hitting on me. My Black King looked up at me and smiled, "Should we get another drink?" That smile brought me right back to him. I kept caressing his leg with my foot. I needed to be in some kind of physical contact with him. I needed my melanin to melt into his.

"You keep that up and you're definitely riding my face tonight. Did I mention I love women with pretty feet?" Heart emojis followed.

"Soooooooooooooooooooo?????" Eyeball emojis followed.

"Mmmmmmmm yeah...I definitely need to taste you tonight. You're so fucking sexy."

We texted each other as we stared at one another across the table. I massaged his dick with my foot. He asked if I wanted to go back to his place or a hotel. We ended up at the Hilton.

"I see what you doing."

"What am I doing?"

"You ass. The way it moves as you walk up the stairs."

"Sir, it just naturally moves that way."

We took the stairs up to our second floor room. He inserted the key card as he pulled me into to kiss me. Another breath stolen. "I definitely need to shower now. HA!"

"Ok. I'll be waiting."

I ripped that damn dress off so fast! I was ready for all the dick he was about to provide me. I was doing a cheerleading routine in my head; I was so excited. As my afro shrank down from the shower steam, I felt the curtain move. My Black King was completely naked, climbing into the back of the tub. I giggled and asked what he was doing. He looked like a honest to goodness God in human form standing over me, then lowering to his knees. "I told you I was going to taste you tonight." My head fell back into the shower water as I grabbed the wall and curtain, moaning for God to come collect my life. He picked up one of my legs, placing it on his massive shoulder and began eating my pussy like no man should be capable of eating pussy. "I need to feel you inside me again."

"Again?" My spirit knew what I meant. His spirit knew what I meant. He was confused. "Again.", he said with a smile, standing up. His dick was a genuine work of art. I licked my lips at the size of the piece of flesh that was about to penetrate my body. Without a condom, absolutely reckless, he pushed into my body, hitting parts of my vagina I never knew I had. "Stop! Did you just cum inside me? I'm not on birth control!"

"No. I didn't. Why did you stop me?"

"What's dripping down my leg?"

"Umm, that's coming from your body."

Cum was oozing down my inner thighs as he grinded that big Black dick in and out of my pussy. Liquid shot over three feet from my body against the hotel room wall. He backed up with a surprised smile. "Shit! This is the best sex ever! Your little kitty is so fat and tight. Fuck."

This Black King moved up and down my slightly toasted melanin like he did countless times in past lives. He perfected his talent with each stroke, each touch, each lick, and each eye gaze from the middle of my thighs. I tell you; I was not prepared for what This Black King was about to represent in my life.

When I left him in the morning, fragments of my mind cried. They missed him so much, but this new body I'm in didn't have the same ties to him. This body I'm in now had two kids she needed to take care of. This Black King held me like he was protecting his Queen with his last breath. His massive arm was so heavy for me to remove from across my person; I had no choice but to wake him. We kissed and that feeling took shelter under the last bone of my ribcage, on the left side of my torso. Over three years later, that feeling shoots physical muscle spasms through my flesh with thoughts of Black King.

The downside of being with This Black King, however? He's a true King. He has fought in war and lived to make it home. He's always steps ahead. His logic and ration overrule all emotion.

His logic and ration overrule all emotion.

He expects his Queen to be the same.

He once told me in a past life, "A King cannot truly lead if he spends all his time worried about his Queen. She should be as fierce and mighty as he is. That is how great relationships work." So, you can only imagine how I felt when This Black King, MY Black King, told me I needed to improve.

I needed to clear up some mental and spiritual shit.

This mother fucker didn't even know I had been writing and figuring out my shit like two years before I met him! He doesn't know me! How dare he tell me I need to improve?! He doesn't know who the fuck I am! Fuck this guy!

I did what any Queen would do for her King; I nosedived into the last dark place within me. A place that has been so guarded, it was wiped from my memory since childhood. They knew he would force me to work on me. They knew he would help me heal. The ancestors sat back and watched how I handled it. They sipped tea and shook their heads in disappointment. When everything bubbled to the surface, I couldn't take it. I wanted to take a step back from this Black King just for a moment. Just to clear my head. He told me he would be there.

That's what he told me.

I was with my husband for nine and a half years and not one time did he ever make me feel like I did the first night I was with Black King. I was instantly hooked.

DICK

MA

TIZED

My mouth is watering just thinking about it.

The downside to a King? Selfishness. Arrogance. Cruelty. Emotional issues that could fill Jupiter. Black King turned into Dr. Jekyll Mr. Hyde. It was psychological warfare. It was like he took on some strange God Complex role with me. Like, he had to "fix" me. I was never good enough. Too bubbly, too short, too much emotion, too soft, I had to "earn" him, "You're fucking mean". I was so confused constantly. I felt like I was in a room filled with smoke and mirrors. I know I was crying on my birthday. I know I was hurting driving away from his home because he was at the bar, when we were supposed to be hanging out. I cried and begged that I didn't want to just be sexual gratification, but I'm here years later broken hearted for the first time in my life.

I was just sex. I gave him that last small piece of me I kept locked away in a tower higher than Rapunzel's.

I was just sex. He told me he loved me and meant it; that he was ready to put a ring on my finger.

He looked me dead ass in my eyes, while pushing deep inside me, "I just want to see you happy, and successful, and protected." I believed what he said to me. I gave him trust.

His smile.

His smile pushed 350lbs. Dumbbells onto my chest and held me against the bed with safety and value. He made me feel like he loved me. He took it all back and said, "I was just caught up in the moment." Why wouldn't he love me? Why wasn't I good enough?

I still fucked him after that...I still let that man fuck me and push all of his emotional issues and need for intimacy onto me after that...

DICK

MA

TIZED

I didn't want to let the feeling go. I gave him all of me. He wasn't willing to give me more than a few hours of his time. He didn't want to just hang out as friends. Black King didn't need any friends. He spoke to me like I was his dog. I was chasing something that would never be. I stopped chasing. Black King emotionally murdered me. I could no longer feel anything. I went right back to Tinder where I met his ass and resorted to the philosophy I went by in my 20's: Best way to get over someone is to get under someone else.

Two

Creating A Roster

Science says women hit our sexual peak in our late 30's, early 40's. I believe science, but I never looked up what that entailed exactly. I definitely should have done some research in advance. At least had a chat or two with some of my older lady friends. I have the hormones of 37 fifteen-year-old boys, seeing porn for the first time. I'm constantly on edge. And after the vaginal beatdown Chicago Dick and Black King provided, I simply could not get enough. Even when I think to myself, "I'm really sick and I may poop on myself if I orgasm", I'm still probably going to masturbate...multiple times. Someone please saves my soul.

And, my vagina.

Black King rationed the dick and toyed with my emotions. Like a little girl begging for her mother's love and attention, I would call and text all the time. I needed him to know that I existed. "I'm going to wish him a great morning." "I'm going to tell him that I hope he's having a great day." "I haven't heard from him in three days. Let me just check on him. There must be some horrible reason he isn't blowing up my phone the way I'm blowing his up."

Why wouldn't he call me?

Why wasn't he tripping all over himself over me?

He would tell me he was busy with the police academy. That he was tired. That he had work. He never had time to take me on a date or just hang out to get to know each other. He had time to fuck me once a month. No matter how clear the signs were, I still went full force lunatic in love, telling myself he was being honest with me and that he was genuinely dedicated towards achieving his goals.

When he fucked me over for my birthday, I was devastated. I simply wanted acknowledgement of my existence. I didn't need over the top gifts or anything like that. Send me a text. Make a phone call. "Hey, I have a lot to do today, but just wanted to stop and wish you a happy birthday, Sexy." That's all I needed. I waited until 3pm. My heart was so angry, I sent him a scathing text message. He didn't step outside of himself to see I was sad. In my mind, it didn't matter that I was throwing a tantrum. It was my birthday and being childish was acceptable to me. He punished me like I was an insolate child raising up against their father. I updated my Tinder profile and met a couple of guys to keep in my back pocket for a rainy day after that nonsense. I didn't know if I would need them. It was nice to have back up plans though.

Once I was able to finally collect myself up of the floor of battered emotions, I put myself together and sprayed myself down in, Au De Beast Mode, to cover the stench of my heart hemorrhaging black sludge. I couldn't take him thinking he could do whatever he wanted to do to me regardless of how much I loved Black King. I needed to show him I loved me. I didn't, however. I had never understood how to love me. I had never taken the time to learn how to love me. I was never willing to get real with myself. At the time, I still wasn't there. I worked hard to act like I was doing big things, put on my big girl panties, and initiated conversations with new men.

Creating a roster is something I never thought I would do. I've never been into sports even though my dad is a fanatic. It just didn't appeal to me. I grew up as an only child and I've always been rather charming. I have never really had to compete for anything. And, the idea of watching grown men sweat and smack each other on the ass over a ball? That's real gay and not the gay that I can take part in, and since I can't have fun with it; PASS! That mindset left me clueless on team building however. So, I built based upon what I had and what I didn't have, I recruited via Tinder, solely based upon looks and body. Vapid Los Angeles type shit. Shout out to my hometown!

Team Tracey 2019-2020 Spring season:

Team Player #1: FriendZone

Blerd: [Blurd] Black nerd.

He's into anime, and wide variety of music is easy for him to discuss. FriendZone caught my attention because he looked like he would be that good guy with moderate quality of dick. The type of dick that ain't gonna blow your back out, but will leave you satisfied enough to keep you smiling in you "Kept" lifestyle. With a white mother and Black father, he loves talking about his disdain for, he is a mulatto that is uncomfortable with his Blackness, mostly hangs out with what seems to be hopeless white boys. FriendZone is one of the kindest men I have encountered. He is an amazing listener. He knows how to communicate effectively. He's warm and loving and incredibly funny.

Average in height, he loves lifting weights. He overdid it however, and now it's just not physically appealing. You know the cartoon musclemen? Yeah...sssshhhhhh!! Don't say anything else! Leave it alone. That's between you and me though.

FriendZone is most definitely a sneakerhead. He has some of the freshest kicks and loves showing them off. He will also sell them for the right price. I enjoyed conversation with him from day one. He resisted my flirtation and forced himself into the FriendZone with awkward goofy responses to things I would say. He always kept me laughing and smiling and feeling beautiful. I was able to open up about Black King and he told me about a younger woman he was dating that wasn't treating him right. He lingered in the shadows, always there to run to when Black King treated me like a peasant. He took me out for drinks and dinner, hung out on my couch and watched movies and drank wine, when I was lonely in my new home. He gave me all the emotional affection I couldn't get from the one I really wanted it from. I really did like him as a buddy. He was a great buddy for six or seven months.

Team Player #2: Dial-A-Dick

The last few months of living with my ex-husband, we continued having sex on and off. He was only nice to me when I gave him some pussy, and I needed to make sure he wasn't going to renege on paying me a portion of divorce money.

Side note: It is sad what women have to do in order to be treated fairly. Fuck!

We decided to spice things up a bit by inviting one of the dads from our son's baseball team over to watch us fuck. I won't describe what Dial A Dick looked like for fear of exposing him, however he was just as cute as his demeaner. Soft spoken, and definitely worked out. There were things that turned me off out him, but the things that turned me on outweighed the negatives. When I first met him, he thought I cooked for a living at the time and asked for my card. That's how conversation kicked off. He talked out his married life. I spoke about mine. When I told him I was no longer committed to my husband; that we merely lived together, he told me how sexy he thought I was and how badly he wanted to stick his dick inside me. He loved how big my breasts were. It reminded me of how much Black King enjoyed my breasts. I was hoping his touch could feel just as good as the man who held my heart. I asked about his wife. He made every excuse as to why he didn't really love her and that because of their situation, it was ok to be a fuck boi and cheat on her. I should not have crossed the line. I honestly wasn't in the beginning. My pussy is a bossy bitch though and that is all I'm going to say about that!

When the night came for all of us to play, I was so turned on. My pussy was dripping thinking about him stroking his dick, while he was enjoying gazing at my vagina being filled up. It never happened. The Dial A Dick sat in the car, then drove away, stating I didn't answer my phone, when I said that man the front door would be open. I had the whole fantasy planned in my head. Then, my ex-husband can't keep it up because he's got damn nervous! I was ready to throw the whole night away. Captain Patriarchy ate my pussy until he was able to get his little man back up and running again. It was a disappointing night, but it was now months later, and I was in a new house with a fat little kitty that needed a beating. I called him, Dial a Dick because I could dial him up any time, and he was going to jump if he knew he could get just a sniff of my pussy.

Team Player #3: Alf

I really had to think about a name for this guy, and "Alf" was the best name. The young kids are going to have to Google this, however, my generation knows what I'm talking about! Alf was from out of this world, but there was nothing "Out of this world" about him other than his appearance. He was such a basic character, and so was this guy. Alf was extremely tall and handsome, but that was really all he brought to the table. He always talked about how women were crazy over him and he couldn't find a nice good woman. He was career driven, brought to this state because athletics. Personally, I've never been into jocks. One of the many reasons I left the Captain was because he was obsessively competitive, and the "jock" attitude that nothing was better than his existence in this world. Again, Alf was tall and good looking though. So, I added him to the team.

Team Player #4: That Tinder Guy

That Tinder Guy was purely accidental. The reason he is called, "That Tinder Guy" was because I completely forgot his name because I deleted his number from my phone after the first night. I met him scrolling Tinder one night as talks of a nationwide shut down were no longer words, and we were elbows deep into a lockdown. He didn't have any photos of himself on his profile. Just random funny memes and a bio in which, I knew immediately, he was Black. He was looking for someone to smoke and chill with. He was getting lonely. I was...dying inside. I needed someone to fill the void of companionship. If he was cute when I met him, I would fuck him to see what that dick was like and where I would place him on my team. If he wasn't cute, at least I had a new smoking buddy that wasn't afraid to hang out during the ramping up of the Rona. Even though That Tinder Guy was the fifth to be added to the roster, the last player is an MVP player.

MVP Player: A player that stays on the roster past one year.

MVP Player #5: Mr. Inconsistent

I had a few on my roster that I had been communicating with for months. My closest friend during this time in my life was on her own Thot journey as well. Neither of us could keep our greedy paws off Tinder. There were so many gorgeous Black men to sleep with. She and I would play "Tinder War" to see who could get the most matches. We got double points if we got a match with someone, we both swiped right on. It became my drug addiction when Black King hurt me. Dealing with my emotions was the last thing I was going to do then.

During a Tinder War session, he popped up. I almost swiped left on him, going through profiles too quickly. His photos were professionally shot. He was well dressed, and dripping with finesse and class. His profile said he was, "Saphiosexual". OMG! SHUT UP! Like, I'm totally smart! Swipe right! Instant match! He super liked me. Isn't that adorable? I sent the first message. At this time, I was thirsty. I wasn't waiting for anyone to chase me. I was a lioness on the prowl. He messaged back almost immediately. We chatted briefly and exchanged numbers almost immediately.

When I tell you this is a man that knows how to sweep a woman off her feet, I mean it! Where do I even start with this sexy ass piece of church going man? He moved here less than two months before we swiped right on each other. His profile said that he wasn't looking for anything, but his face definitely told me I needed to sit on it. Our conversation started off cute and innocent. He spoke about helping a church in North Alabama on the weekends. He grew up in a God-fearing household of church musicians. He plays instruments and sings like a song bird. I loved how intelligent he was. Words flowed so smoothly from his soft lips that I have rarely kissed. He was engaging my mind as well. Fuck. I was begging the ancestors his dick would be just as good.

Assistant Coach: Ashley Madison

If there was anyone to go on a hoe journey with, this woman was your TOP pick! She had started before me by cheating on her husband. When he found out, he didn't fight. He simply minimized himself further and allowed her everything. He was a good man truth be told. She actively worked to make him seem useless in the house. When it came to parenting their children, he was the typical stand around dad. You know, the one that properly provides for his family financially, but tends to look like a statue in the corner of your life in every other aspect. I felt sorry for him because that Bitch was a mutha fuckin wild animal behind closed doors. She worked so hard to be a Boss Cougar, following in the footsteps of her grandmother. She turned her nose to men above the age of 30. The idea of dating a real man grossed her out. She romanticized a grown man personality in the body of a 21 year old. Like, a 70 year old pedophile man eyeballing an 18 year old girl, she looked at younger Black men like the Pokémon. She wanted to catch them all. Ashley Madison is her name because she seems like the good-hearted blonde lady that doesn't see a person's color, down the block. Ashley is a heartless whore with little self-worth at the core. She would fuck and suck damn near anything walking to feel any type of connection to someone without giving her heart away.

The Perfect Thotiana. She will bust down on 'em!

She was intrical in the success of Team Tracey. She was me and I was her. We were codependent upon one another because neither of us knew how to stand on her own.

I rolled over that morning needing him inside me. My vaginal muscles were pulsing. My hole was leaking. My pussy was like an unused Slip N' Slide, waiting for his little big boy to come play. He was sleeping hard. I covered my head with the blankets as I slithered my tiny body down against the lower half of his. I licked my lips and wrapped them around his limp dick without my hands. I sucked his dick back and forth in my mouth until he woke, moaning from pleasure. "Fuuuuuckk…"

"Do you like that, Daddy? Do you like how my lips wake you in the morning?'

"Fuck, yes."

"Good, Daddy. I love to please you. May I sit on your big Black dick, Daddy? May I feel you grow inside my wet pussy?"

He refrained from verbally expressing his desire for me. He spoke to me with his hands, using them to pull my frame onto straddle his lap. He slowly sat me down on his dick, pushing inch after inch inside my short vaginal canal until you could see the imprint of his dick just below my ribcage. As I grinded my pussy against his scroctum, my muscles clamped down on his big juicy meat, and he pulled me in tighter.

"I love you." My womb spasmed with pleasure, and my mouth spasmed out those three words over and over.

Black King couldn't hold back. He growled, "I love you" in my ear as he pulled my heart closer to his. He held me like a caveman claiming the prize woman in the village. I left my body. I looked down at us sweating in the heart of winter. I needed his words to be real. I needed to be loved so immensely. Those words from his mouth claimed my world.

I wish I could be lying next to his body now. To be able to have him close enough to lick his melinated flesh.

In less than a month of bickering for submission from me, and me relentlessly fighting against a man I knew, at my core, didn't want me past sex, that bliss turned into him insinuating that I was sleeping around.

"Can I be honest with you?"

"Yeah! I would prefer if you were always. lol"

"The last time we fucked, your PH was...off."

"Ummm, I felt like I had a yeast infection coming on. Maybe that was the reason? I don't know. I haven't slept with anyone other than you..."

"Un huh. Well, I went to the doc and he said I was ok, but gave me antibiotics just in case."

I should have taken this as a warning sign then, but I had been out of the dating scene for ten years, and even prior to being with my ex-husband, I lived as an open lesbian! I didn't know...I didn't think.

"If anyone gave someone something, it would be you giving it to me, Buddy."

"If I gave you anything, it would be clamydia. That's treatable."

"Treatable or not, I made it this far in my life without Pussy Cooties. I don't want to start now!"

SO, NOW THERE'S SOMETHING WRONG WITH MY PUSSY??? I had had enough of this man; this Black King! It's time to test out the new players on Team Tracey! Fuck you, Black King!

Three

Tryouts

"Dear God!! Remember me telling you about Absolutely Not?"

"Who's Absolutely Not? LMAO"

"Well, his sister died this morning. He called to cry on my shoulder. What am I supposed to do?" He was the one talking about taking me on some trip overseas."

"Omg that's awful!!! But I still don't know who he is lol. That's a tough call because you don't want him to think there's anything more to the relationship, but you obviously don't want the dick."

"I don't have a picture of him. We have been talking since the end of October. I met him Classic week. We don't speak often. Only been on two dates. Definitely don't want the dick. He's a cool friend though."

"And no sex?"

"Ew. No."

"Then you should support him. Maybe bake or cook something an bring it to him? Lol ok."

"You would have known if there was sex. LMAO Even if it was bad, you still would have known."

"HAHAHHHAHAAHHAHHA"

"Like, I want to invite him to my gumbo party, but there's a chance Black King may show up."

"Yeah...no."

"Look at me over here being petty and messy."

"For no damn reason!"

Ashley Madison and I played with men like little girls played with Barbie Dolls. We tossed feelings and emotions to the side. We couldn't have the men we wanted to be with, so we lived in disillusion with a hard heart, good pussy, and head game that would make you think Jesus feels something awfully special of you. Ashley was knocking Black men out like the slave trade! Chile, when I tell you her team was going to the World Series that year, if there was a world series for hoes, truer words had never been spoken. I mean, scientifically, the vagina is a muscle, therefore, her pussy was weightlifting champion of the world! She was taking beatdowns from dicks bigger than us put together like a Transformer! Come on being more than meets the eye!

I'm over here talking shit about her enveloping cooter mouth. I don't know how I can walk. Let me hush and keep this story moving along.

Ashley and I pumped our heads up on a regular basis. You really couldn't ask for a better one to make you feel top notch. She was there from the beginning with my Black King. She watched me fall and stumble over love continuously with him. She didn't judge. She knew how it felt to love someone that would never love you back. She sat beside me through the good and bad. It didn't matter how many men I chased. Black King was all I wanted. Any chance I had to have him in my space, I took it.

"Girl, that Nigga mad because I kicked him out for getting mad at me because he fell asleep and so did I. It ain't my fault this pussy put him to sleep."

"GIRL! YOU have done a number on him! Lol"

He could turn off his emotions just as I could with others. Years later, I still don't know how to stop loving him...I haven't figured out how to not want him around all the time...

Black King loved me hard, then went back to putting me in side piece status to a relationship he didn't even have with someone. How did I become a side piece to nothing? Let's start Team Tracey Tryouts...

I crossed the line. It was completely my fault. I was drunk and high, swimming in a pool of my own tears. I wasn't thinking correctly. Had I been confident in myself, I'm sure we would have never slept together, we would still be friends to this day. My insecurities and need for someone to show me I had value overpowered my basic logic. I made a huge mistake and lost a friend. In my defense, he definitely made it weird in the end, and that's what really killed it, but I will admit the part I played.

I asked him if he enjoyed giving head. He immediately responded.

Thirsty ass.

This is one of the reasons he stayed in the friend zone for so long.

He said it's his favorite thing to do. Really, Sir? Well, well, well...Guess who has a poontang that needs to be licked??? I asked how long it would take for him to get to my house. I also gave a list of disclaimers.

TRACEY'S DISCLAIMERS:

This shit is crazy. I know it is, but I have always had sexual issues. I never knew how to articulate them nor did I know where they came from. Black King brought all my underlying issues to the surface with the safety he brought to my life. He triggered years of childhood memories I repressed my entire life. I was forced into a corner having to admit molestation that shaped who, and how I dated and valued myself all these years. I learned how to have sex at 39 years old. From not allowing anyone except Black King to kiss my neck to asking men to not wear cologne when they are with me. I refused deep penetration, no kissing during sex, no laying their entire bodies on top of me, no attempts of dominating me; I had all kinds of sexual disclaimers.

FriendZone said it would take 45 minutes to arrive and he was cool with my sexual hangups. I double checked to make sure he was cool with just eating my pussy. I was horny, but not willing to fuck him at that point. I told him I just wasn't ready for another man's dick. I poured another half bottle of red wine into my glass because I'm classy like that, and waited for him to arrive. My roommate at the time opened the door for him as she was leaving. FriendZone slowly opened my bedroom door wearing an off white colored jacket. What's funny is I actually used to own a jacket just like it. Go figure! It was so cute. I should have asked him if I could have that jacket. He probably would have said yes...regret.

Completely intoxicated, I was laying on my bed drinking my glass of cabernet or shiraz. It definitely was not a merlot, but my wine is typically red. I laid without a piece of clothing covering my body. A little alcohol will have me thinking I'm the queen of the world. I wanted my pussy licked like the last ice cube in Hell. "Well, don't you look ready?" He said to me as he walked through the door. He was right. I made him wait more than six months. I wasn't wasting anymore time. He better shut the fuck up and get on his knees before I change my mind. Sometimes, talking can really kill a mood. He was walking a fine line.

FriendZone was in his 20's with no kids and no intentions of ever having children, probably because in so many ways, he's a child. "You got your glass of wine." Ok Detective Donald, thanks for the observation. Let's go, Bro! He takes off his jacket and his shirt as he lowers himself closer to the floor. FriendZone popped back up to crawl towards me to kiss my face. Wrong lips, Dude; you're kissing the wrong lips. I gave him a quick peck on the lips, against my desires and he definitely noticed. I had no wanting for any type of intimacy. I gave that to Black King and only him. He moved between my thighs with a slight side eye. I closed my eyes as I felt that warm wet tongue slide in the middle of my labia majoras. "Mmmmmmm..." I giggled and pressed my lips on the side of my glass to drink my wine as he drank from my vagina. I was honestly shocked at his capabilities of licking the puss puss. It was just right, and he didn't give up until I came down his chin. When I felt his tongue inside my vaginal canal? Done. Fin. I needed that release.

When he was finished, he laid next to me. I did not invite him to do that, but since he had just finished tongue fucking me, I guess I could talk to him for a little bit. And, since he was there, he should definitely massage my lower back. We ain't finna just be laying here like some couple. I handed him the jar of Muscle Relaxer, (www.calibamaorganics.com) and asked politely, "That was great! Would you mind rubbing this on my lower back? Please?" "Sure." He's really simple like that. I proceeded to take two more sips of wine, and then turned over onto my stomach. As he pressed his hands just above my tailbone, I began shaking my ass just a little. I couldn't help myself. I blame liquor. His breathing went deeper as he grabbed onto my hips. He wanted to throw that dick between my cheeks badly. The pressure in his grip told me so. "Ok, I can't do this anymore. I'm going to go."

"Oh. Ok. Thank you for coming over." I didn't know what else to say. It's not like I was going to ask him to stay anyway. At some point, I was going to kick him out. He saved me from having to tell him to leave. I grabbed my wine and continued drinking as he collected himself. "Are you going to walk me to the door?"

UGH! I WASN'T PLANNING ON IT! I'm drunk and just came. I really want to go to sleep at that point...

"Huh? Oh...right! Sorry...Hey, will you take my trash out for me?" If you know anything about me, I hate taking out trash. I'm happy my son is old enough to do it now. I've managed to only take out trash three times in almost four months!

"Uh...yeah...sure..." He didn't seem like he wanted to, but he was already going outside anyway. I ran to the kitchen to give him the bag and told him where to drop it off. I walked him to the door and even gave him a hug.

I texted Ashley, "Girl, I just got some bomb ass head from FriendZone. I made him give me a massage. He couldn't take it, so he went home to jerk off. *high five* Now, I'm home alone watching Netflix with a smile on my face."

"AHAHAHAHAHAHAAHA What happened to Black King?"

"Fuck him. I'm tired of the emotional games he plays."

I thought we were cool when he left my house. Again, before he even came over, I made sure he was ok with only giving me head. The next day I get a text saying, "I don't want to be the sexless side Nigga with good head..."

Oh shit...I almost threw my phone across the room when I read that.

I thought to myself, Sir, please have a seat while I explain something to you. You need to be on tip top shape of your head game in order to slide into my phone making stances and shit. And, you're not. This half Negro had most definitely lost his whole ass mind talking to me with that kind of base in his voice. I had to reiterate that we discussed him only giving me head. Sex was never on the table. Not once. I was kind in not telling him his tongue action isn't what he thinks it is. I didn't want to deal with my own emotions. I wasn't going to deal with his in that moment. I ended up walking away from the conversation right after I ensured I could still get some head in the future if need be. I had already found someone earlier that afternoon before FriendZone arrived. I had options, but I wasn't trying to burn any bridges. Head with nothing in return is hard to come by and my Mama didn't raise no fool.

Clearly, it's time to put Mr. Inconsistent on the field. Let's see what he can do. While he's warming up, I'm still scouting Tinder each day. I mean, what team only has five players and an Asst. Coach? None! What team only has the first five players selected without even going through tryouts? None. You're like, "Touché", huh? I know.

He told me he was in North Alabama when we matched on Tinder that day. I told him he had to stop by El Cazador Mexican restaurant while he was up there in Huntsville, AL. It was my favorite Mexican joint in Bama. That is what connected Mr. Inconsistent and I; food. He mentioned he was there the day before and planned on picking it up again on his way home for research purposes. "Would you like for me to bring you anything back?"

"OMG!! Are you serious??"

"On one condition- Would you have dinner with me?"

Smooth, Brotha. Straight smooth.

"I would love to."

I gave him my order and headed over the next evening, once he arrived home. His head was far larger in person, but his body. Good heavens, I craved licking every tattoo and Fraternity branding on his body. He was so calm and friendly. He warmed up our food, poured some wine, and turned-on Harlem Nights. We laughed and added commentary to the movie. I made a comment about racial politics and that's where I solidified his interest. "I have never heard a woman speak so bluntly about that topic. That shit is sexy." Shifting to music because we stopped paying attention to the movie, I got up to dance to the song playing on the radio. He said, "What? You know how to dance? I love to dance! That man jumped off his couch so fast, grabbed my hand, and preceded to one two step and spin me around his living room.

When the song ended, we laughed and high fived. I felt bright and vibrant in that moment. Black King didn't provide experiences like this. He had only seen me playfully smile outside of the bedroom once. Mr. Inconsistent was about to fill my longing for affection. He was about to make me feel valued and appreciated. I hugged him. He hugged me back, then looked me in my eyes as he picked me up, wrapped my legs around his waist like a belt, pushed me against the wall and kissed the breath out of me momentarily.

That was one of the most panty stealing moves I had ever encountered.

Next thing I know, I'm lying on his couch spread wide open, with his words muffled between my thighs, "Got damn...why you taste so good?" I don't think he really meant for me to answer that. "I stay hydrated." I could have at least thought of something better to say, but there you have it. "I want you to sit on my face."

Yup. He's a definitely a keeper.

After 40 minutes of riding his face like the last ride of Paul Revere, I leaned forward on all fours. I just needed to breathe for a second, but I couldn't. Mr. Inconsistent went tonsils deep trying to suck my soul from my asshole. He didn't miss a second. He pushed my ass up higher in the air, parted my cheeks and ate my ass like he was Jesus eating the last piece of sliced bread on Earth. This preacher's boy was praying to The Father via my anus. I was tingling my toes. Can you tingle toes? I thought my eyes would stay permanently crossed. He picked me up, both of us completely naked at this point. Where did his clothes go? How was he able to get naked and I didn't notice? He carries me to his bedroom, passionately kissing me the entire time. His dick was so got damn thick...I wanted it, but I still wasn't ready to actually have sex with anyone after Black King. The head I got that night? It had me thinking very hard about changing my mind. I told him I had a lot of sexual issues. He understood and didn't ask me to touch his dick one time. He feasted on my vagina for hours. My legs hurt from shaking and cumming so much. I hadn't received head like that since a woman I dated when I was 28!

I couldn't stay. I had to leave. Motherhood was calling. I had to get up early the next morning to take my son to his very elite private school. "Your pussy tastes so good. I want to taste you all night." If I had any emotions at the time, I definitely could have gotten caught up with this guy. I was thinking about making wedding arrangements for a second. We laid together as our heart rates went back to normal. I began putting my yoga pants and tank top back on. He stood in front of the door completely naked and begged me not to leave. "Just let me taste you a little more." I'm ready to call that man right now, based solely on typing all of this out and thinking back. "I have to go. Let's see each other on Thursday."

"You want me to take you out to eat? Where would you like to go? What would you like to eat? Whatever you want to do, just let me know. I have a meeting in the evening, but I can meet you after."

"You can come to my place, if you like."

"Sounds like a plan..

Why do men always offer food as a way of getting vagina? Like, what desperate bitch is out here fucking for meals? Girl, if you don't go get some self-esteem!

I walked away with a smile that could shine light in heaven!! JESUS!! I looked back and he was still standing in his doorway with nothing on except a rock hard dick waving, "See you soon, Girl".

Thursday could not come fast enough!! I made sure the father of my children came to pick them up on time. Those kids had to be out of this house by 6pm. If I had to take them myself, them Half Negros wouldn't be in my home.

"BITCH!!!"

"WHAT BITCH?"

"BITCH!!!!!!!!!!!!!"

"BITCH...WHAT????"

Ashley sent a bunch of eyeball emojis to show the high level of nosiness she was about to elevate to. I told her all about my night with Mr. Consistent and sent her a few screenshots of conversations we had. "I love how his name still isn't saved in your phone. BWHAHAHAHAHAHA"

See, that's some more of her business...

"Girl, this Nigga in his feelings now."

"FriendZone? Girl, I told you."

"We over here having conversations and shit because I didn't do anything to him, AHAHAHAHAHAHAHAHAAHAHAHHA"

"You opened Pandora's Box, Girl."

Mr. Inconsistent shows up over an hour late with an abundance of cologne on to cover up the day.

SEXUAL DISCLAIMER:

Like I mentioned earlier, I cannot do fragrances of any kind, other than deodorant. I have learned that I have sensory issues with smells that refer back to childhood sexual trauma. Strong smells cause me to tense up and feel unsafe. I can't relax. I feel like something is being covered up and hidden. I didn't realize this until 39 years of age. I have never been able to completely enjoy sex because I didn't know this about myself. It definitely makes me wonder how many other people have these underlying issues, never having an answer as to why they feel the way they feel.

Anyhoo, back to Mr. Inconsistent… He tells me that his meeting ran late and he apologized as he flopped down on my couch, overtly exhausted. We briefly spoke about his day and mine. That's cute and all, but that's definitely not why I invited this man over. Two days prior he told me he was into my personality and racial and political views. "Your profile said you weren't looking for anything."

"I wasn't until now."

Boy bye. Stop it. Why do men lay it on so thick? Like, didn't I just let you get tonsils deep in my vagina already? It should be apparent that I'm on the same page of just wanting to have to fun without anything else. Why make women feel like there's a wedding ring surprise if you're not going to call after a few times? I didn't understand, but at least I knew what was going on this time around.

He complimented my appearance and smiled so softly into my eyes. His lips pressed against mine as I slid my hand across his jawline. We moved into a zone as our kissing grew more and more intense. Mr. Inconsistent laid me back on my couch, created a "V" for victory with my legs and the cunnalingus began. Lick. Lick. Lick.

I wonder if he's awake right now. Nah…I'm not going to call him…

"Fuck you feel so fucking good. Put your fingers inside me."

It was a done deal after that. He hit that release valve and I squirted all over him, the couch, the rug, the floor. I wish I could have taken a picture of his face when he realized my vagina did tricks. He made me do it again with his eyes stretched as wide as humanly possible. Did he think he is going to get a closer look if his eyes were open more? He looked like a 12-year-old excited about the last splash drop on a Magic Mountain water roller coaster! I had to stop myself from laughing. He stood me up after the second time, "That shit was so fucking sexy."

His dick was out. I couldn't resist the temptation to, at least, stroke it a little. Oh fine! Since my arm was being twisted, "Do you have condoms? I want you to put this big ass fucking dick inside me so much."

"I don't have condoms."

"Go get some."

As soon as he leaves, I grab a bottle of Bombay Sapphire gin and grapefruit juice and put back three glasses, poured half a large bag of bougie pork skins down my throat, and posted on Facebook, "If he leaves to go get condoms and actually comes back, he definitely wants it."

I texted Ashley, "Girl, his dick was so hard! I told him, 'Go get condoms. I wanna feel that big ass dick slide up inside this pussy. I'mma be waiting for you with this ass in the air ready to take it.' Bitch, when I tell you he put them pants on so fast and ran out that door! LMAOOOO"

"Mother Fucker doing 100 all the way to the store! BWAHAHAHAHAAAHAHAHAHAHA"

25 minutes later, I'm drunk, we have condoms, and he's now in basketball shorts and a wifebeater. We immediately went to my

bedroom and took off whatever clothing was preventing us from rubbing naked against each other. His dick was so fucking hard. He didn't need any time to warm up. The hook on that man's dick took out my vagina! When he growled after I squirted all over him again, I zoned out and pictured Black King hitting my spot. "Fuck me, OMG! I want this dick all the time!"

"You can have it anytime you want."

My reality was blurred from the alcohol. All I could see was my beautiful Black King. Nothing else existed except him and I. I could feel the way his hands would hold my hips as he used my body like a rag doll. I could see the way he would smile down at me. The sensations he once made me feel, I began feeling as I envisioned him through the eyes of someone else. "I'm about to cum again." This was that final orgasm for me. You always know when it's time to tap out, and that was the moment. Mr. Inconsistent, snapped that condom off and came all over my creamy tan ass. I loved it. His warm cum dripping into the crease between my ass and thighs, as he breathed deeply. He fell down onto the bed, "God Damn."

I know. I know...

I went to the bathroom to clean myself up and passed out next to him. Of course, right after I made sure he knew he would have to leave early in the morning. He was actually going to the gym and hour earlier than the time I gave him. It was perfect. The way he was talking about getting to know me better and me being marriage material scared me into thinking he was serious. He could not lay up in my bed and catch any kind of feelings. If Black King decided he wanted to be with me, I couldn't have anyone lingering around to screw anything up. I was so desperate for that man to love and value all of me, when I couldn't do it for myself. I would tell myself I was trash. I was a loser. I was old and divorced and broken and damaged. That's how he made me feel, except when he was on top of me. Except, when he was looking into my eyes. Except when, he was so deep into my body, I could feel him pushing my internal organs into my shoulders. Except, when he wanted nude photos of me.

That smile.

Why couldn't he love me? What was wrong with me? I would have given him anything…why wouldn't he love me?

When Mr. Inconsistent left, I smoked a blunt, drank whatever liquor was sitting in my cup from the night prior, and went back to sleep. I woke up to check a text from Aunt Sug and immediately text Ashley. "Girl!! My friend out here just texted me a cop was shot in my area. I have been blowing Black King's phone up!"

"OMG GIRL! SO SCARY!! Is he ok?"

"It wasn't him. My heart dropped, Ashley. I couldn't imagine…"

"Girl…"

"I'm still gonna fuck Mr. Inconsistent again tomorrow though. That nigga ok. He wasn't even involved in the shooting. I ain't shit, Bitch."

Ashley and I spoke in emojis, gifs, and screenshots half the time. The next fifteen messages were in gif form. With all the dick and tongue action he was offering, why call him Mr. Inconsistent? Because he was never consistent after that. He didn't show up the following night. He fell asleep, he said. Then, ghost…for a while…Ugh! Someone put Dial-A-Dick on the mound! Let's see what he can do.

Four

Switching Out Players

Putting together a solid roster was much harder than I anticipated. Like, I don't understand how men have gone this long throughout time boasting of the glory between their thighs, yet there's always some issue, if not multiple, that they gloss over with shiny arrogance. I will never understand for the life of me how anyone would want to be claimed by the average American man. Junk food, TV, white supremacy, drugs, and the internet has taken its toll on this third world nation. Please send aid. We are not ok.

Two weeks after the disappearance of Mr. Inconsistent, my hormones were shooting off more missiles than an Obama presidency! I was feeling desperate and wanted a good ass dick down.

"You're emotionally needy. You needed me to fall for you because you need to feel control over someone. It ain't even me specifically. I'm just convenient. You can't fuck without emotions. You can say all you want. You act like my fuckin' son when he doesn't know how to process what he's feeling. It's fucking stupid. You avoid shit, say dumb shit, don't make sense, get angry, place blame... your dick just ain't worth this shit, man. I don't even give a fuck no more. Damn."

"...Tell you what, we should just cease conversation. As much as I love those tits, I'll pass. You stay in your lane, I'll stay in mine. You have a nice day."

"I think I made that clear. Say less."

"Great."

"You and your control issues. Lol."

He reduced me down to my breasts. I would say that really hurt, but I was so numb and angry at that point, it didn't matter. It was just a hurt little boy throwing a tantrum like Captain Patriarchy. If it wasn't Black King emotionally berating me, Captain was keeping a list of money I owed him such as $26.83 for windshield wipers. $100 for Chinese New Year. I'm not even Chinese! Why do I have to participate? $8.97 for Netflix...I would go back to the family house to wash clothes or tend to my garden only to look at petty nonsense like this on the fridge I picked out for my culinary needs.

I needed release from the consistent Single White Female drama my soon to be ex-husband was providing. When he sent me a text message saying the divorce was going to, "get messy", I didn't anticipate him calling the cops on me for coming into a home, equally ours, to wash my clothes. I still had most of my personal belongings in the home. I left because I couldn't take the fighting and arguing and lying. And, watching him sneak out of the house with his sad little backpack, like I didn't know what he was doing was embarrassing. I was offended because I cared enough about him to be open and honest with him. I genuinely worked to be friends with Captain Patriarchy after seperating. It didn't matter. He wasn't getting this "his pussy" anymore. I was no longer under his control.

I sent him text after text, "You can always sell the house and split the equity or buy me out. Send back the divorce negotiations." It was literally that simple. Every time the cops showed up, they told him, "If you don't want her here, you need to get a court order. This is legally her home too."

Nothing mattered. His man feelings were shattered on the floor. The Captain when over the deep end. Calling the cops was just the beginning. It escalated to snooping around my house, while I was at the grocery store. It was using our son's key to my house to enter my home and search around. I watched him walk around my living room and dining area from the back bedroom, thinking a serial killer had come to the hood to dismember me, and it's this crazy Chinese man I had kids with...why did I have kids with this man? Why?

I cried hard that night, while hugging my bong for dear life. I sent FriendZone a text.

I was hoping FriendZone would offer some decent pipe since his head game was good enough to make me cum. I still had worry on the brain, so I told him I just wanted head with the possibly of sex. "Bring condoms just in case."

When he showed up, I was ready to go. He got undressed and I can assure you, his body did not look the same as it did two weeks prior. His muscles were so cartoon like. It was weird, but my hormones said, "Bitch, if you don't get on all fours, so you can't see him and bust one out really quick!" My hormones had full control over me and they are heartless. He laid down next to me and tried to longingly stare in my eyes; Awkward. "You know what? Want to know one of the reasons I held off on having sex with you?"

"Why?"

"Because I thought you would fuck me like a white woman."

"Well, that's racist and what does that even mean?"

"It's not racist. Maybe it's a little prejudice, but definitely not racist. And, you know exactly what I mean."

"I mean, I actually kinda do know what you mean, but explain it more."

"Like, I really thought you would have sloppy jack rabbit sex with me. White women like that shit for some reason."

It's so weird. I don't understand how they enjoy having a man just bang their bodies against their private parts. What kind of pleasure is that? No rhythm, no passion, no soul, just bang, bang, bang, bang. Blagh. Vomit. I want no parts of it.

"What??? NO! Who even has sex like that? I would never do that."

"Whew! I was really worried." He extended his hand to grab the back of my neck and pull me in for a kiss, but I have intimacy issues. I automatically bobbed and weaved away from him. Mike Tyson would have been proud of those speedy skills. "I just want straight dick. I don't want to kiss. Will you eat my pussy first?" Why was he so insistent upon treating me like we go together? Sir...

"oooohhhkkkk..."

He ate my pussy until I said, "Gimmie some dick." To which he tried to put on the condom, but was having trouble. WHaaat is going on, Jesus? "This has never happened before...I'm having a hard time staying hard." I thought about all the times Black King told me if I didn't like what he was offering, there's the door. As I begrudgingly looked at this wiggly, ashy skin noodle hanging from this man's oddly shaped body, I couldn't help but to think, this was not the next door I planned on standing in front of. It looked like a deceased sea snail out of its shell. How did I end up in that situation? I was so hung up on proving something, anything to a man that didn't really give a fuck about me, I was lowering myself to anyone just to feel something, even if, for a brief moment in time.

You know what I have learned that I despise? Men that need time to "warm up" and complain about it. They never care when we aren't ready. They don't care to take the time to get us wet, so we don't feel like we are getting rug burn on our vaginal walls because you're trying to shove your non lubed piston into our socket hole. But we have to care about your big baby feelings? Alllllll the fucking time, we have to "be gentle/Oh, the tip is sensitive/not so hard/can you suck it a little?" Close your eyes stroke that dick until it stands at attention, and let's go dammit!

"Just rub your dick on my pussy. I'm always wet. Trust me." I got on all fours like my hormones told me to and thanked everything holy I was at least extremely stoned through it all.

"I don't think that will do...oh yeah...that did it"

SUCCESS! We have hard penis!

Well shit, I thought his dick would feel better than that. He was so bland sliding in. It was such a letdown. I was so pissed when he did exactly what we spoke about before having sex. He humped on me like a jack rabbit for less than ten minutes before going limp. "I finally figured it out. You're not sexually attracted to me."

Fuckin' duh Sherlock Holmes.

"What? Right now? You're doing this right now? It's not that I'm not attracted to you, I'm just not comfortable doing a lot of things sexually." All of which was the truth and a lie at the same time. No regrets. "Can we finish? Is that possible?"

"Ohhhkkk...I'm happy that I'm going through this right now, so we can talk and work through this. I can't get hard again. This is just so weird."

Weird? Brotha, you just busted faster than you realized and you are actively working to play this shit off.

I'm not talking about a got damn thing! Those are your issues, Sir. As he began talking, I turned on my side and pretended to fall asleep. I was not going to deal with any of what was about to transpire. He finally stopped talking and realized I wasn't paying attention. He put his clothes on and tip toed out of my house. As soon as I heard the front door close, I grabbed my phone to text my best friend aka Ashley, and told her about the fuckery that had just taken place. She laughed until she cried.

She's cold blooded. I just wanted some dick.

The next morning I texted FriendZone, that he should have woken me up to say goodbye. I didn't mean it, but whatever. He immediately began talking about his feelings, "I'm trying not to be all Drake about this..." But, he was. I joked about him being in his feelings. He said, he's working through everything, so he'll be ready next time. I'm not training wheels! There would be no next time. You don't make me cum, we ain't fucking again. No. I don't have to because I don't want to. Next time...boy bye.

I didn't let him come to my house after that. We maintained talking on the phone and texting. About a month after that uncomfortable night, he built up courage to ask to come fuck me. I told him I was on my period, having bad cramps. My pussy was just as blood free as an 80-year-old vagina. I couldn't bring myself to tell him I didn't want to fuck him again. He said he forgot I was on my period that week and that he had been tracking my menstrual flow.

Excuse me? Sir. WHAT?????

We are not together. We had sex one time. Why was he tracking what my pussy did? I didn't even track that shit and it's attached to MY body! I couldn't even offer a friendship after that. It was just too weird. I stopped answering his means of communication. I didn't even care why he was doing it. I didn't need an explanation. I just needed him to disappear. Six months or so later, he randomly reached out.

Ignore.

Ashley and I were always on the prowl for new younger men to fuck. She had a Black King of her own, but the call of the hoe game was too loud. "Look, there's a bunch of rocks you have to break on Tinder. But then, when those rocks break, you find diamonds. By diamonds I mean fine ass Black men with big dicks, STAMINA, good head game, and ready to fuck." We needed something, anything to deflect from the pain and hurt we endured loving men that were not willing to give the same in return. There are moments where I look back and see the joy we brought one another. Mostly, I see the fountain of self-hatred we encouraged each other to swim and frolic in so carelessly.

"I don't know...Maybe I just need to sit my ass down and focus on getting my shit together."

"You can do that and get fucked right! Why can't we have it all? Why do we have to keep limiting ourselves?"

My Asst. Coach made a good point. Why can't we have it all? I come from a far away land called NosyAsHellia and grew up in the providence of Fuck-Around-And-Find-Out. My wanderlust for life is too great. And, I lacked self-control on all fronts. That's why I couldn't have it all at that time. I wasn't planning ahead to make sure my company stayed afloat during the modern day apocalypse looming around the globe. I wasn't making sure my savings stayed in my savings. I was making up a personalized sexual sports team! If one player didn't make the cut, I was negotiating team tryouts with some rookie I swiped right on. I blew through so many Tinder profiles, there were days the app told me, "You're all caught up!" Excuse ME? Thanks for adding to the level of pitiful I had fallen to, Tinder.

Swipe right. Wait for them to engage first. Ashley said she never messages first because that's desperate and you never want to seem desperate. But...I was though!! I wanted good dick on a consistent basis until Black King realized I was his queen. What if the guy I swiped right on was playing the same game and he was waiting on me to say something first because he's just as equally sexy as me? I don't care what Ashley says! I'm the head coach of this team. If they are a 7.5 or above, I will only wait two days for them to say something. Your fine ass ain't getting away from me Cat Daddy! At some point we are going to be laying naked together!

I sank to a new low each day during the year of our Lord and Savior, 2020. I couldn't explain how much my divorce and Black King were draining my joy. I couldn't explain how I was allowing it to happen so freely. Yet, there I was, a shell of a woman, pretending to be unstoppable. I put men through an online "Application process". How well did they engage in conversation via messages? Are they actually typing out words or am I getting, "wyd"? Do they know the difference between, "Their", "They're", "There"? Are we going to spend the entire time talking about the woman you expect? Are we going to spend the entire time talking about how you are a leader, except you don't have a car at the moment, so you're going to need me to, "Come pick you up right quick"? Are we going to talk about what you don't like about me? The process was intensive, but the line was long. I was only keep the best of the best...and, the not-so-great...and, the ain't-shit-brothas...Ok, I was keeping 80S%, but they were in tiered categories of qualifications, at least.

One man would fail grammar in the application process? Switching him out for the guy who claimed he loved eating pussy was a no brainer. He was going to add value to the team. If one gentleman aced conversation, but seemed like the dick was trash? He's going to be replaced with the 27 year old that smokes great weed, lays pipe like a warrior, and texts, "Aye, wyd tho".

Well, let's see who's next on the field. I called Dial-A-Dick.

Five

I Don't Even Like Sports

"I want some dick."

"Damn. Damn. What position you like?"

"Sir, I'm nasty. I like all of them."

"Lmao. Sooo what's up?"

"I mean, I have my kids, so I can't leave. You can definitely come over though. We just have to be quiet."

"Ok. If, I sneak out, I can't stay long. Is that cool?'

I swear I scream laughed when I read that last comment he made. Years later, I have feelings, but I still laughed again, when I typed that. He can't stay long... I didn't want you to any fucking way. Did he think I was going to ask him to spend the night? Get the fuck out of here...

"I was going to put you out after anyway. We ain't creating a relationship, Bruh. hahahaha I just want some head and some dick."

I gave him my address; told him I was impatient and didn't like to wait. Then, I texted Ashley!

"Girl, I'm about to get some dick, and I'm not even changing the sheets from last night."

"I just cackled like a witch! WE AIN'T SHIT, BITCH!"

"Now, let me go hide all these used condoms deeper into the trash can. I don't need no one asking me any kind of questions I don't plan on answering. I'mma make him take out the trash after he leaves too."

"I love you." Ashley then sends me a screenshot of a man messaging her on Tinder.

"What are you looking for? I'm looking for a friend, woman, lover in that order. Someone that have a lot to offer. Come with her own, good credit every relationship i had i took care everything which a man should do 75% I need a woman that can help me make executive decisions. Not just a pretty face or eye candy i need more than that.

A friend, woman and lover in that order instant connection."

For the life of me, I will never understand why men have the sheer audacity to type shit like that to a woman and think we are about to drop everything in our lives because you just proved you're worth it. Sir, please leave this planet if you have typed this to a woman to start off a conversation. You don't deserve to get pussy. You deserve to sit in a corner, in a stone building, on the edge of Planet Jackass and speak with a therapist until you learn how to behave like normal people.

I said what I said.

"Omg BLOCK"

"Blagh!!!!!"

"Right?! My clit is dry as fuck reading that bullshit. The very first message lol"

An hour later, Dial-A-Dick was at my front door. Clearly, he was able to turn his car into an airplane and fly to me. I have strict rules about men being around my children; You ain't. I don't need my kids thinking every man I meet may be their new potential stepdad. I don't want to put them through getting to know a man, only for him to end up being a fart in the wind within six months to a year because their mother refused to give real love in a relationship. They didn't deserve to go through that. I was that kid and it was torture. Woman after woman moving through my dad's life. Man after man rolling off my mother. Dial-A-Dick was different though. He personally knew my children. If they woke up and saw him there, they would have thought nothing of it. They would have asked about playing baseball or signing up for the next season.

I quietly walked him from the front door to my room. WHYYYYY is he wearing so much fucking got damn cologne? It makes no sense to walk around smelling like the masculine version of Bath and Body Works! Sir! What is the absolute problem? What do you really smell like that makes you think you have to wear *that* much cologne? Sir, you are causing folks to pass out and dead people to wake from the grave! I think Jesus himself might be able to smell you. Please stop doing this. Also, are you using your wife's lotion? Why do you smell cherry berry flowers blossoming in the fucking spring? What the entire fuck is going on???? Let me open all the fucking windows before my kids wake up, thinking I am baking fucking sugarberries.

As we walked into my room, I took my robe off and laid back on the bed. He made no effort to kiss my face. I was happy. He rubbed my skin a bit, then leaned back to present the world's most veiny penis. Ok, ribbed for her pleasure! Not putting it my mouth though. Nope. Gross.

He quickly undressed, put the condom on and got down to business! I was so physically tense from the amount of cologne he had on, I couldn't calm my anxiety filled brain down. Dodging and diving his neck kisses, "Oooh yeah, you getting this dick deep". I clenched my vaginal muscles like the doors of Fort Knox. I refused to let that man lay there and think he was gonna fuck me like I was his woman. He was absolutely absurd. "You so fucking tight. Got damn." I took myself to a different place mentally. I could no longer be present. I wanted to cum, and make him and my trash disappear out of my front door.

I went to one of the lives my soul lived with my Black King. We were richly melinated royalty, so dark we would not be seen at midnight. Our bodies rolled in flowing waterfalls of crystal-clear fountains in our palace. Every kiss he provided my body, his lips spoke, "I love you, my Queen." I could feel my tiny stature bleeding onto his torso. I deeply breathed until he slowly took away each breath I had. My King pumped that massive piece of flesh into any body cavity he so chose. I belonged to him. He could have it all. Every last drop of my body.

I came four times, popped back into reality, then got the fuck up off the bed to go clean myself up. "Oh, so, you done done?"

"Yeah. I have to get up early." I was not about to lay around with that mediocre stroke any longer than I had to.

"Can I lay here and beat off to you?"

"yeah...that's fine."

I put on some music and began to dance while touching myself. He was going to get the fuck out of my damn house! Wasn't he the one talking about he couldn't stay long? If you can't stay long, why are you trying to stay longer? You can sure go home and give that nut to your woman. Within five minutes he muttered, "Damn...You sexy as fuck", nutted, and was in the bathroom cleaning himself up, putting on his pants. "Can I get a high five or a fist bump or something?" Fuck, why are men so got damn needy for half ass accomplishments? Who made you feel great for being average? They need to have their ass beat. You can have this trash bag put into your hands. That's what you can have. I asked him to take out the trash on his way out, as I gave him a side hug, which he had no problem with, and he took his condom with him. Honey, I don't know what he was thinking. I promise I would never try to trap him after what he poorly did to my body.

Dear Jesus,

Please bring me some quality dick. I deserve it.

Your Daughter in faith,

Tracey

I needed thoughts, prayers, and any other positive energy anyone could give off. This roster is falling to pieces before I even have a chance to put it together. What the absolute hell was going on? I thought dating would be easier than this. Ashley and I were blowing through men like the Rich white kids blow through cocaine. Within two months, we had accumulated over 500 dick pics and endless thirsty ass messages begging for a subtle scent of our panties. We didn't wear any though.

"I just texted Mr. Inconsistent, 'I can't wait to fuck you tonight.' He gone text back, 'Take it easy on me'. Nigga, if you don't shut the fuck up and put this pussy in your mouth!"

"Ugh! What is wrong with these men?"

I was happy to have Ashley and she was happy to have me. We were the best and worst people to travel down the heartless road of love together. We encouraged each other to be the best at being our worst. We broke heart after heart with smiles on our faces. We cackled at men yelling at us for using them for sex. We didn't care. If you couldn't offer us respect and value, we couldn't offer anything other than wanting no more than what dangled between your thighs. We numbed ourselves with bottle after bottle of alcohol. Gin being my go to, in order to keep my waistline in check, but she preferred a good lager.

I had knocked a few guys back, but was still at square one. This is why I don't like sports. Just when you think you're winning and you puff your champion chest out, the ref throws a flag on the field and next thing you know, the scoreboard tells you, you're a loser. I didn't have my Black King, I still had my hurt and pain, I still had my shitty ex-husband pulling petty move after petty move to trigger all my emotional anger towards life, and you know what else I did not have? Someone to love that felt the same for me. I was still losing and I couldn't see reality through the toxic liquid smeared into my eyes. I didn't want to feel, unless it was my Black King.

As we moved into the beginning of spring 2020, The Rona loomed in the air. Was it going to stay in China? Since when does a virus go around like, "Nah, I ain't going to America. They got too much bullshit going on." Fears mounted surrounding the future of my very small, but growing body care company, but I had little savings. "Hey, may I have a $100? I don't know what's going on with this Covid shit, and I need groceries for the kids."

"I can't afford groceries for two households."

What the fuck is this man talking about? It's still the same four fucking people. Just because we don't live in the same house doesn't automatically add extra mouths to feed. You fucking bitter, pink skinned woman in sheep's clothing. I couldn't stand my ex-husband. I have never been attracted to a bitch, and here I was fighting with a bitch for leaving his bitch ass because he does bitch ass shit.

Let me go find some dick and some liquor, so I can zone out of reality.

Mr. Inconsistent cancelled again. He had back-to-back meetings about the future of his job with the possibility of a global shutdown. Meanwhile, my ass is buying bottles of liquor for Black King to show him, I was happy it wasn't him that was shot. Looking back, someone needs to shot off one of his testicles. Fuck him.

I sat on my therapist's couch crying my eyes out. Even though I saw her once a week, I was still doing dumb shit with complete recklessness. I think about what would have happened if I wasn't seeing her? Would I be even worse? "I want you to describe what kind of fruit you are."

"What? Fruit? Ummmmm... A thick juicy watermelon. I love watermelon. It quenches thirsts by offering maximum hydration. Watermelon cools you off on a hot day. Will sooth heartburn, so its fucking healing, and it's just as sweet as it wants to be when ripe."

"Now, describe what type of fruit Black King is."

"He's an apple. They are healthy for you and useful, but isn't going to make you do backflips of delight and joy unless it's in pieces, served hot, with ice cream on top; basic at the end of the day. You REALLY have to like apples in order to enjoy them."

"You're poetic with how you describe how amazing you are, but you get so angry and hurt by people that aren't what you want them to be. An apple is incapable of being a watermelon. Stop trying to make that apple a watermelon. Just find a watermelon."

I was willfully ignorant towards my actions. My insecurities were based upon how others viewed me. It was hard for me to see things outside the scope of direct logic sometimes. I was extremely forward and direct. Because of this, people assumed I didn't take their feelings into consideration, but I do so deeply, I ended up beating myself up and tearing me down. I pushed people away not understanding how to except people where they were.

I was begging someone to make me better and I just wanted to wallow in my hurt and pain. The Pity Train always serves the best drinks, and God knows, I do enjoy a good cocktail. She said, "You know how amazing you are. When are you going to feel that?" She spent an extra hour with me that day. My life was such a fucking Telenovela. She definitely earned every dollar she made being my therapist. That poor woman probably went home after each session, ripped her clothes off, then laid in a hot shower, in the fetal position to cleanse herself of the sins I committed. Bless her heart, y'all. She is a strong woman! That was my last session with her.

Talks of a global shutdown rumbled like an earthquake building momentum. Days were beginning to become worrisome for me as I was concerned about the amount of money I had in the air for markets I booked over the coming months. I was not good at social media marketing, so my online sales were not my money maker. I enjoyed being in front of people and talking to them directly. I wanted them to have faith in me, not only what I was selling. Talk about allowing insecurities and low self-value holding you back in life! Am I right?

Unfortunately, I was...

I began drinking more and gardening as days became warmer and spring was approaching. Every time I thought of my Black King, I poured a cup, wiping away tears. Forty-five minutes prior to Captain Patriarchy picking up our children, I would increase the amount of liquor in my cup to ensure I would be intoxicated as they were walking out the door. I didn't care about anything after my kids were gone. I just wanted to drink, fuck, garden, and sleep. Ashley was pretty much the only reason I was coherent some days. I stayed sober enough to text her, and scout on Tinder for my next team member.

Maybe I should have looked into fencing? That's a sport that requires only me and one other player. Team building is hard. I'm pouting like a five year old.

Six
The World Stopped

Ashley was better at hiding her emotions than I was. She had a man she wanted to be hers just as badly as I wanted Black King. He treated her like a girlfriend four days out of the week, but when he wanted his time, he wanted his time. Ashley was extremely emotionally needy. She needed CONSTANT stimulation. I have absolutely no clue how she was able to be good at her job, chase after that young man, and have the hoe game on lock! She was a got damn professional! But, definitely not the professional that should be training anyone or aiding in their success. We were damaging to one another because we refused to acknowledge just how broken we were.

I was explaining how men worked to her often. I'm not putting my nose in the air when saying that either. Understand, the knowledge I was giving her were the words out of Black King's mouth. In many ways, he became my man interpreter. I was relentlessly confused at the backwards ass; stupid shit men would do on a regular basis. Grown men acting like puberty surged little boys, shouting that they were leaders, demanding a woman follow him blindly. If you can't even articulate the difference between a feeling and action, I promise, you won't be leading me down any path you have laid out.

"Why don't they not want to boo us up? Doesn't he know I'll give him the world Lol. I would, Bitch…I would…I'mma keep blowing through men until he comes around". Ashley wanted that man so badly, she needed him. I could always feel it in how she spoke about him, but she rarely showed genuine emotion.

"One monkey doesn't stop no show! Now, I want some dick. Good dick makes everything better."

"It really does."

I had all this extra time on my hands as the world began to make preparations to close its doors. I wanted to fill it with all this good ass Black dick I was experiencing for the first time! Dear sweet heaven on Earth! These corn and potatoes fed Southern men walk around with their heads held high in their stupidity and toxic arrogance because they gone shut you up with that DICK. I never understood why women lost their minds over these imbecilic children. Then, I got knocked out by Black King.

The cravings I would have when I needed his body pressing against mine. The anger and frustration I would display. Yelling and screaming, "I want some DICK! Why can't you just be fucking normal, so you can fuck me right!?" I didn't care that I sounded like a lunatic on steroids. My vagina wanted to feel him slow stroke his way to my heart, calming all of my anxiety. I was incapable of being calm and exposed. My sexual experiences leading to Black King were riddled with fears, doubts, insecurities…The only time I could feel anything was when I was with him.

That smile.

I could never get away from the feeling his smile brought me. It washed away all my pain, even if for only a few hours. "I love you. I love you. I love you...I want to see you happy, and protected, and successful...mmmmmmmmm" Each time I touched myself his voice played over and over, hoping one day, he would mean it.

I needed his poison to become my remedy.

Please love me.

I'm scared.

Please Love me.

I'm so hurt.

Please Love ME.

See me.

Hear me.

I don't know how to say it correctly.

I don't know how to get there.

Hold my hand.

Hold my body.

Please Love Me.

I constantly begged. The more he pulled away. The more I lost my mind.

"Hey. Good morning beautiful."

Is this man for real? He's GOT to be joking me! He just ghosted me a couple of weeks ago, but we supposed to act like nothing happened?

"Where have you been?

He sends a video of him rubbing his dick. And, that's what made me tune into the conversation. He proceeded to tell me how he contracted the Rona! I couldn't believe it. This deadly nightmare disease was this close to me. But, like, he's alive. He had a few more days left of quarantine, but said he felt normal. "I really want to lick that pretty ass pussy then you squirt all over my dick." A fully nude photo followed.

"LOL Why you want my pussy?"

"Quit playing. Your pussy is so good, even you want your own pussy."

Touche, Sir! I do enjoy pleasing Aunt Patty.

I needed to feel desired so badly, I risked contracting a deadly disease because this man pumped my head up the right way. I have a strong immune system. We seem to have the same quality of health. If he can survive, so can I. That's what I was telling myself.

"Bitch, I'm about to go to Mr. Inconsistent's. HAHAHAHA"

"BITCH! WHAT!?"

"Yes, Bitch! He got the Rona, but he's pretty much ok. If we fuck from the back, we kinda six feet away, right? And, a condom? I think I'mma live."

We took nothing seriously.

As Mr. Inconsistent opened his front door, I began pulling my jade green mini dress over my head, and walked through the door way. "Why do you have clothes on? You knew I was on my way."

"Uuhh, I thought I was supposed to be the aggressive one?"

"Sir, are we arguing or fucking?

"Shit, the way you talking, we fucking until you drain my nuts."

"Good answer. Now. Take off those clothes and get on your knees."

He grabbed my neck, firmly with caution, took me down to the floor, and licked my pussy until I came on chin.

As I sat up, "Let me ride that dick. I want to feel it in my stomach."

He rolled over and I climbed on top. My pussy devoured his big dick over and over, until I dug my nails into his neck and looked into his eyes.

"Oooooh, you gone make Daddy cummmmmmmmmmmmmmmmmmmmmmm..."

His eyes rolled into his forehead, he stopped breathing momentarily, then gently pushed me off him and curled up into a ball on the floor. I came. There was nothing else for me to do there. I went to wash up, put my dress on in the opposite direction of how I took it off, and slowly walked out of the house as he was sitting up and coming back to life.

I called him two days later. I wanted a little bit more. He went on about feeling like I only wanted him for sex. What was with guys and this shit? Every time I turn around, you have your dick out to be worshipped and praised like we are in the house of the Lord, yet as soon as it's turned on you, there's a problem? You knew I didn't like you as anything more than fucking you when I needed to be touched. I had no intentions of meeting your mama or your friends. Boy bye. He stayed in his feelings and refused to give up the dick.

March 16th, 2020.

The World stopped.

What didn't stop? Tinder, liquor stores, the police, the fire dept, all first responders, trifling mutha fuckas, people living on the edge, and social media. I had my kids week on and week off with their father. I had all the men in the neighbor, along with their friends, driving by to watch me sunbathe and garden in tiny bikinis. They would take turns bringing bottles upon bottles, and a variety of weed. Letting me know, if there was any type of drug I wanted, they would happily provide. I woke up to a cup of coffee, then drank and ate off the land all day. I set up a hammock to take naps in and a shower to cool off under or take a piss. I went in the house to shit and cook meat pretty much. I felt like I was living in a happy dream world.

My ex-husband began falling into volatile hatred towards me. He would call the police, refraining from telling them I was his Black wife, in a white city. He would act like I was some insane Nigger baby mama in the South+. I never in a million years would have thought I would have children by a man that would use the police as a weapon against me. I never thought I would be viewed by the police as a respectable, good mother. Captain Patriarchy pushed boundaries and limits, working hard to make me look unfit. The harder he worked, the worse he made himself look.

As I was chatting on the phone with Ashley, watering my garden, the Captain pulls up next to the curb near my back gate. "Bitch, here comes this silly mutha fucka."

"I cannot with you! Why does he have to be a silly mutha fucka...wait. Don't answer. I know why. LMAO"

He was supposed to be picking up the dogs and leaving. He just had the kids less than 48 hours prior. I told my children that if their dad came to the door to not open it. I expressed they just saw him. He wasn't stable. I didn't trust that he would try and remove the kids from my custody. His logic and reasoning had slipped into a Blackhole.

"Can you hand me the dogs please?"

"No. I'm watering my garden. You're capable of picking up those dogs, putting them in your car, and driving away in silence."

"I don't want to step on your property. You told me I wasn't welcome anymore."

"Because you broke into my house! Of course, you aren't welcome. You can get these damn dogs and leave though."

"I want to give the kids a hug."

"Dude, get the dogs and go home."

The Captain finally walks into the backyard to grab the dogs. When he drove off towards the front of the house, I thought that was the end of that. I thought I wouldn't see him for another few days. I was wrong. I went in the house to check on the kids. Something felt off. Thank goodness I put the chain lock on the front door that the kids couldn't reach. Covered in absolute insanity, that fucking man parked in front of my house, and went to the front door to manipulate my children to open the door for him! So, we are just overstepping my parenting now? Just fuck me?! I said don't open the fucking door! I said take those fucking dogs and go the fuck home, and your Asian monkey ass is on my got damn PORCH! What the hell was wrong with this man? Who the fuck was this man becoming?

"Get off my porch, Captain!"

I made sure the kids were calm, then I went back to watering my garden in the backyard. Less than ten minutes later, this lunatic is walking down the sidewalk on the side of my house and my kids have their shoes on, walking out my back door!! I am in full blown rage at this point.

"ARE YOU FUCKING KIDDING ME? WHAT THE FUCK IS GOING ON?"

"YOU CAN'T KEEP ME FROM MY KIDS, TRACEY!"

"No one is keeping you from your kids, you fucking maniac! You just had them! YOU are currently keeping them from me during MY time with this bullshit! GET THE FUCK AWAY FROM MY HOUSE!"

I yelled at my kids to take their asses back in the house! This man had me so mad, I was cursing at my children that were being played as pawns by this moron. The mental and emotional damage he was causing didn't matter.

Nothing mattered except his ego.

I hung up with Ashley and called my lawyer. I refused to call the police with my kids there. Their dad had done it too many times already. They didn't deserve any of this. My lawyer told me to walk around to the front of the house to see if the Captain had finally made his final disappearing act. Alas, he was standing upon the second set of steps that led to my front door with his back turned to the house. He was focused on texting someone with anger, physically, turning his skin red. He looked up to see me on the phone. He must have assumed

I was calling the cops. He was such a fucking BITCH! After all the times he called the police on me for no reason, he shouts, "Real grown up, Tracey!" He finally shuffles to his car, gets in, and I stand there and make sure he drives away from my neighborhood. I went back inside to calm my kids down once again because their dad was on his bullshit...again.

He was weak and wounded. He kept the master bedroom as a shrine, never moving so much as the blanket left on the bed for months after I was forced from my home. He changed the locks, refused to negotiate the divorce, refused to be cordial, stalking me, stalking men I would date, calling for welfare checks to see whether or not I have left my kids home alone to get them removed from my custody...I never thought I would see that man that broken. I never wanted to see that man that broken.

I worked to keep the appearance everything was ok. His anger shook life from me each day.

"I don't love you. I didn't really mean it."

I LOVE YOU! I GAVE YOU ALL OF ME. I GAVE YOU WHAT I HELD ONTO FOR 40 YEARS...I LOVE YOU. I LOVE YOU. I LOVE YOU. I cried and sobbed until my face was swollen. I called Ashley, screaming at the top of my lungs. I was swerving on the freeway. I couldn't believe Black King would do something like that to me. What adult takes back love? How do you take back love like it's a Swingline Stapler? HOW? I couldn't take any more games with my heart. I was on complete overload. I had no coping tools for this shit. The spiral began.

I called Alf. I actually sucked his dick unlike the rest. I felt like putting forth this effort meant he would stick around. I allowed him to spend the night and sleep in hospital pants I had stolen from one of the many hospital stays I've had to endure becoming a mom. I wasn't soft and mild, but I did try to be, "Lady like", if you will. I apparently didn't do a very good job. He acted like if we had sex again, he would get the Rona and then he would die after giving me moderately average penis. I was offended, personally.

Then, there was Phillip, but his name was Frank, but he introduced himself to me by his middle name, which was Albert. I didn't like Frank or Albert, so I renamed him. I enjoyed Phillip much better.

"Bitch! LMAO What the fuck is wrong with you? Phillip?"

"Yeah!! It sounds so French, right? Like, when we fuck, I can think about this gorgeous Imported man pouring himself into my American body, filling me with all his 'culture'. HAHAHAHAHA"

That's what I had in mind. Then, I ended up fucking Phillip. He was such a mild Dad of The Year kind of man. He loved having family time and working on home projects. He made dance videos with his sons and worked out. He said all the right things and showed me he was marriage material.

Fucking vomit.

However, I needed the validation of someone looking at me like they wanted to put a ring on my finger. We chatted for a few weeks before meeting. He wanted to get to know me a bit before actually being face to face. What a sweetheart, right? Phillip arrived dressed like the hip dad holding onto his youth at all costs. Everything from the hat to the shoes matched. Had I been capable of feeling something for anyone other than Black King, and had I been looking for one of the most kind average man ever, Phillip/Frank/Albert would have been such a great catch!

We sat next to one another on my couch. I gave him about a half hour of small talk and fake laughter before initiating sexual play. I helped to move his hand under my dress. He fingered me until his dick got hard, slapped the condom on, and I got on top. Three minutes in, he nutted and howled like a wounded woman in the night with his eyes shut tightly. I looked at him disappointed until he opened his eyes. Then, I quickly smiled, booped him on the nose and said, "I told you I had good pussy." He laughed, flipped over and ate my pussy, until I sent a waterfall splashing across his face. He jumped back in complete shock, knocked over my bong, and I grabbed my phone and walked into my back bathroom. I immediately started texting Ashley.

"Bitch, like a werewolf? He was howling like a werewolf? I'm crying over here!"

I called her just to make the exact noise he made. It wasn't remotely like a werewolf. At least you can somehow picture a sexy werewolf howling and it will turn you on. This was a sound that maybe, like, a walrus would make, if you could imagine a walrus fucking and having the best orgasm of its life, in the highest pitch walrus "growl". Do walruses growl?

Anyhoo- I will make fun of that man for the rest of my whole entire life. I make all the promises. If I was on my death bed and I had to think of a funny way to go out, this memory would definitely cross my mind.

"Bitch. I'm so fucking mad about my bong. I had that damn thing since I was 21!! He better not be in my house when I come out of this bathroom!"

"Wait?? You've been in the bathroom this whole time????? TRACEY????"

"FUCK YES! I have. No shame. Zero. It's been exactly 46 minutes. He better have some sense in 46 minutes that he needs to GO with that simple ass dick, breaking shit in my fucking house! MAN! FUCK HIM!"

"HAHAHAHAHAHAHAHAHAHA!!! HAHAHAHAHAHAHA!!! HAHAHAHAHAHAHAHAHAHAHAHA!! I CAN'T BREATHE!!!!!!!!!!!!!!!!!!!!!!!!! HAHAHAHAHAHAHAHAHA TRACEY! BITCH!!!"

I walked back out to my living and that silly mutha fucka was still in my got damn house! He at least had his clothes on. I sat down next to him, not acknowledging he was there. "Well, I guess I will go."

"Ok."

"Are you going to walk me to the door?"

"I mean, it's literally right behind the couch. This living room is small. Do you really need to be walked to the door. I can see you from the couch."

He carried his head low and walked out the door. I saw him two times after that because he wouldn't stop driving past my house talking about, "My Mama live up the street, and I saw you outside." It was two times too many.

He never offered to replace my bong. Never; not once. That's really what it came down to. I really loved that bong and he wasn't man enough to handle good pussy, and he fucked up my shit! At least, offer to replace it! I thought Southern people were supposed to have manners? I'm not going to lie though, I did call him months later to pretend to be nice and act like I wanted to hang out. It was because I needed some construction work done. I couldn't afford to pay full price for a legit contractor and I knew he was rebuilding his home on his own.

I definitely would have listened to that howl one more miserable time to get my floors fixed. I would just make sure he was nowhere near glass.

Ashley sent me a series of memes:

"You know who's really gonna suffer during this social distancing?

Dudes on dating apps

Welcome to courtship, Brad.

Welcome back to talking to a gal for WEEKS prior to meeting.

We're pen pals now, my dude.

We bout to get Jane Austen up in here.

Now, write me a poem."

"Do not go to a man's home for a hookup right now. You could get quarantined there and they don't even have sheets. If they don't have sheets, they definitely don't have toilet paper. Maybe one bag of hot pockets. A can of Cheeto puffs/. That's all you'll have. Is that what you want?"

"You know why I love single moms so much? As soon as their kids leave, they fucking!"

"You were nose deep in her asshole after one dance at a nightclub two weeks ago. But now, if she coughs in your direction, you're ready to slap the life out of her for trying to give you Covid."

I laughed via text message. I was waking up from a drunken slumber. I didn't know what was going on most days at this point and I was less than a month into a global shut down. How could all of these men be so defective? Why do we glorify these oversized children so much and excuse always all the dumb shit they do because we want our internal organs pushed into our rib cage. It's sad really.

My Black King's voice rang through my head: "You in the South now, Baby. We sweep things under the rug down here." I swept my feelings under the rug no matter how much I needed to confront them.

Then, I met Tinder Guy.

Seven

Like, Like Liquor...

Had he slowed down, we could have had a good relationship. That Tinder Guy was looking for some cool person to hang out with. I was looking for a cool person to fuck. We chatted on Tinder for a bit before exchanging Instagram information and phone numbers. He just seemed absolutely regular, and I was excited! He said he didn't have the Rona, he has weed and a bottle, and doesn't start drama. I invited him over.

I was beyond baffled four hours later, sitting on my couch, drunk and high, and The Tinder Guy hadn't tried anything! Like, am I that weird? I couldn't fathom he enjoying my company. I was made to feel like my worth was tied up in how good my pussy was. I made myself feel I was nothing more than vaginal muscles. I didn't care however. He was going to show me what his dick could do.

Thirteen minutes later, he showed me and I was not amused.

"Are you...did...did you just cum?"

"Yeah? You didn't?"

"Did it look like I did?"

"I mean, I was trying really hard not to look at your face, so I wouldn't cum fast."

"It's only been thirteen minutes. What are you talking about?"

"Really? It felt much longer. Are you clocks working?"

"Fucking what? Can you get it back up?"

"Uhh, that's gonna be a no."

"WHAT??? Aren't you 32? What do you mean no?"

"Really? Age? We are bringing age into this?"

"I can't believe I'm having this conversation...Can you at least finger me until I cum?"

"Uhhh, nooooooooooooo...Like, I'm very done. I was just planning to come hang out. I didn't think you were going to put Jesus pussy on me."

"Ugh, you can leave now."

"Like that?"

"Like, why would it be any other way? You didn't provide dick that was good enough for you to stay."

"Damn."

"That's what I said when you nutted fast."

Who's fucking next? I knew at some point in time, I was going to find some good dick. I just needed to keep putting my pussy out there. Aunt

Patty was going to get her needs met; somehow, someway. Dick was being thrown at me left and right. I cannot state enough, the amount of dick pics I was able to accumulate in such a short amount of time. Some men didn't even tell me their real name before sending a photo of how Peter was paying Paul! I would say hello, and BOOM! 12 photos of one dick at a different angle. There were good days and bad days, but at least the bad days weren't so bad, when the good days were so plentiful.

As I drank my coffee with Kahlua, flipping through my affection collection of dick, I look up and who is driving his ass by my house slowly? Black King. I thought he didn't love me? Why is he by my house? This is crazy. I called him. "Why are you driving around my house?"

"I'm working, Tracey."

"Yeah the fuck right! This isn't your beat!"

"Some shit went down. They needed extra coverage."

"You can drive through another fucking street! Don't drive next to my house stalking me, hiding behind your job! Drive past my house again, I'mma be fucking your partner on my porch!"

I didn't even know what partner I was talking about. I was just making threats because my feelings were hurt so badly. There was nothing healthy about the way I handled things with that man. Not one time did either of us offer genuine affection outside of being physically connected in moments of our souls reuniting.

He drove past my house in his unit, after his shift three more times.

"Stop driving past my house! I know when you work. You're not even supposed to be in my area! You don't want me remember? REMEMBER WHEN YOU TOOK YOUR LOVE AWAY? DO YOU FUCKING REMEMBER WHEN YOU KEPT SAYING IT OVER AND OVER, WHILE I SOBBED UNTIL MY NOSE WAS PLUGGED? I do! I remember..."

"Mannn, stop. It's going to be ok. You don't need to yell at me. That's not me. It's another cop. He looks just like me. We even have the same last name."

"You have an identical twin, that is not blood related, that just so happens to be a cop also, AND works at the same precinct as you... Do Birmingham women really fall for dumb shit like that? Like, you're saying that to me with confidence. It could only mean, you have said dumb shit for so long, yet no one has bothered to question you because you so damn fine. That's the only excuse that you could use to say something that absolutely fucking dumb, to another human, at your age."

"I'm not lying."

He was lying. I mean, fucking duh, right?

I found Chef Dad Belly on Tinder that night. He came over after his shift working at a raggedy restaurant about an hour away. I wasn't expecting him to have such an untrained body. He looked like he was about 5 months pregnant on stick legs with long locs. We walked straight to my bedroom. He licked a little. I sucked a little. I was pretty disappointed, but I was drunk and barely coherent. I laid there and let him hump me from the back until I came. I moaned periodically to make him feel like he was doing something. He screamed, "She can take dick!" and we high-fived one another. He said he was going to come back the next day. I called. He didn't answer. We never spoke again. He was just like taking a shot at the bar on a lonely night. He was shoved into my system to ease emotion, and once I was sober, he was gone.

"Do you even know how to play with pussy?" I should have never asked that little boy that question. I probably scarred him for life. He was only 21. I knew he was young, but I was lonely and unexplainably desperate. You can't fuck a baby when you have good pussy. They are either going to fall in love or you are going to emotionally fuck him up. "What are you talking about? You don't like having your clit rubbed on?"

"Um, of course I do. You scratching records though. You ain't playing with pussy. I thought you said you could give that pipe? Let's try that because your hands feel like razor blades on my labia skin."

Looking back, those may or may not have been the most encouraging words.

"Damn…Ok…" He pulled out his dick from his oversized jeans and laid back.

I sat up looking at him. I didn't understand why he was about to take a nap. "Uhhh, are you going to sleep?"

"No. I was waiting for you to suck my dick."

"You gone be waiting a long time. I never said I was going to put your wiener in my mouth. I don't know you like that. Just pull on it a little."

"It's fine. I'mma rub it on your pussy then shove it in."

Gross. He did not have enough base in his voice to be talking to me like that. He wasn't rubbing any of that immature flesh stick on my skin raw! "I'm not fucking you without a condom. I don't work like that." He was so disappointed he couldn't feel like pussy raw. I wasn't. I would have zero regrets if things kept progressing the way they were.

That poor little child tried so hard to get his little homey to stand up. He was so defeated; it just wouldn't happen. "I'm going to get my vibrator. You can fuck me and I can cum. Maybe it will help you get hard." I didn't care about him getting hard one fucking bit. I just wanted to bust one out real quick without having to do the job myself. I grabbed my lucky charm from the top drawer and handed it to this little boy after I spit on the tip. He slid it in and out of my pussy, while hovering on top of me. "Make my pussy cum. Fuck yes." As I was about to release, he tries to stick his raw dick inside me. THE ABSOLUTE FUCK?? I'm going to have to start all over again! He's going to want to stick around longer in order to finish a job he almost completed! WHY ARE MEN THE WORST??? I just wanted to cum.

"Dude, I was about to nut. I told you I wasn't fucking you raw. Please finish."

Three minutes later and some serious focusing, I managed to push out a little orgasm like a meth head pushes out a little terd after a 72-hour drug binge; its small, but does the job and makes you feel so much better.

"So, uhh, you think you gone let me slide through again and make you cum?"

"No. You didn't make me cum. My vibrator did. I can do that myself. Please lock the front door when you leave."

"Umm, ok...bye? I will talk to you later?"

"Bye. No. You will not talk to me later. Have a great day." I swear, that was embarrassing for the both of us. Why would I... why would he want to continue anything with me after that?

Frat Boy Slim? Romeo, Romeo! Where for art thou Romeo? When I tell you I miss this young man with all my spirit, I mean it! If he ever reads this and knows that it's him, I hope he comes to look for me, so I can fuck him at least one more time.

Ten more times.

Thirty...A hund...I don't even want to put a number on it. Daddy touch my body again and again! I was high and awake at 2:30am. I just wanted some good dick. Please Lord! I have endured all the mediocrity one can endure. I opened the Tinder app, lit another blunt, and started scrolling. Left. Left. Left. Left. Left. Left. Left. Left. Left. Left. Left. Left. Left. Left. Left. Left. Left. Left.

SWIPE RIGHT! I almost jumped in the air. I had age minimums. He was 26. Fuck boundaries! I want all of that chiseled warm brown skin all over me. When it was a match, I felt like I had just won a game show. I immediately said hello. He responded back immediately. 30 minutes later, he was walking into my bedroom asking, "Ma'am, may I eat your pussy please?" I was completely taken away by his manners, and his head game. Yes Daddy, I mean young man, I mean PRAISE THE LORD FOR BLACK FRATERNITIES!! What the fuck do they teacher these men behind closed doors!? Father God, he didn't even ask me to suck his dick, he got down on his knees and gave his best impression of what a vibrator would feel like on a clitoris, while he stroked his dick hard. I was so turned on, I let him fuck the everything out of me.

"OMG! Why is your pussy so gooooood??"

LIKE, LIKE LIQUOR... 83

"Make you wanna put your whole body in it, huh?"

"I want to live inside you."

He threw his head back, grabbed my hips with his hard manhood throbbing inside my vaginal canal. He flipped me onto his lap and he went backwards onto his back. His dick jammed into my internal organs and I squirted so hard, I had to change the sheets and mop the floor after. He fell asleep on top of me. I couldn't believe I was letting him cuddle me. I couldn't believe I allowed him to fuck me like that! How DARE he send me to the Lord during all the dead hours??

"You can stay as long as you like. If you get hungry, let me know, and I'll cook you something before you leave."

I have no clue who that woman was. That was Aunt Patty talking. She wanted to make sure Frat Boy Slim stayed around. I didn't disagree. I never wanted to let that dick go! He became my regular in the middle of the night, when I was fiending. Sometimes, two or three nights a week.

Not too tall, not too short, gently shy, kind, soft spoken cool guy swag; That was Frat Boy Slim. Every time he came over, he came with condoms, great head, impeccable dick, good weed, and would fall asleep afterwards. He never brought drama. My pussy did tricks for him. She constantly wanted to show how much she valued what was in his pants; big, fat, juicy, Black dick. I need that dick today! Every day. Honestly, if people had the sex he and I had, the world would be a much gentler place. His sex was always a recharge of joy. We made porn together, recording how beautiful his richly colored dick slid in and out of my creamy coral pussy.

He loved when I wore red lipstick. It turned him on the see the color smeared across my complexion as he fucked my head in the pillows from the back. I would talk to him for brief moments before sex as time went on between us. On occasions, it felt like he fucked me with passion when he knew I was feeling sadness and longing for Black King. His stroke would make me forget everything. It was like taking pure uncut ecstasy. It was smooth, and penetrating. Deep and spirit shaking. He treated my pussy like he was applying to get into heaven. Professing how beautiful I was to him, "I love looking into your eyes when I nut. It takes me to another world."

There was never an encounter I could complain about. He was so amazing to me.

He could have been my consistent dick with no attachments.

I couldn't stop loving Black King, and I should have never created that secret Instagram account.

I should have kept my pee shooter in my pants.

I should not have checked my messages.

"Hey!"- 3wks ago

"Hello? What's going on? - 3 wks ago

"Are you really ignoring me?" - 2 wks ago

"Was my dick that bad?" - 2 wks ago

"Damn...I guess so..." - 3 days ago

Is this guy for real? He really thought we were gonna be buddies after that thirteen-minute shit show he put me through?

"Hey! Sorry, I completely forgot I gave you this account. It's not my main one, so I never think to check it."

"WOW!"

"Wow, what? I said sorry. Anyhoo- Yes. Your dick is horrible. I wasn't intentionally ignoring on here though."

"WOW!"

"Why do you keep saying 'wow'?"

"I'm bored. Want to smoke and hang out though?"

"Yeah, that's cool. You can come through."

I was lonely. It's not like Black King could come smoke one with me. It's not like he would if he could...

I don't know why, but I took some sort of strange pity on That Tinder Guy. He knew his dick was trash, but he was so confident in who he was as a person, he didn't give up on a friendship. He came over. We smoked. We drank. We watched TV and music videos on YouTube. I was loose and care free. I began telling him about Black King. He patiently listened to me. Once I stopped rambling, he chuckled and said, "Put your dick away, Tracey."

I screamed a mighty scream. Dare I say, I scrumpt! It was absolutely hilarious to me! Put my dick away? "What does that even mean?" I couldn't stop laughing. He looked in my eyes, "Put your dick away, Tracey. You know exactly what I mean. If we were in a relationship, I would be the only one with a dick. You can't have a dick with me. I'm sure he feels the same way." I couldn't fathom the idea of allowing someone to have control over me. That's what I was hearing him say to me. I needed to submit. I needed to bow. I needed to be less than myself in order to retain companionship. He showed me what he meant however. That Tinder Guy showed me what it felt like to be loved and uplifted correctly.

He showed me when he put a bunch of extra channels on my tv, so children that were not his could have more options. He showed me when he came over to spend time, not to have sex. He would randomly cash app me money. Always showed up with something in his hand. He consistently checked on me. He cared about me. We rarely had sex. It was rarely good and never long enough. He would typically tap out around the 5-7 minute mark. He put forth his best effort, however and some nights were lovingly magical and fulfilling. He always opened his person to allow me to come to him. He was always on bended knee ready to provide a healing love. I fell for him too. We were together at least three days a week. He offered the safety and security Black King said he wanted for me. The sex stopped being so important. The affection was surreal.

There were days when I was lonely. I wish things didn't go the way they did. I became frightened by the emotions. I couldn't handle feeling something for anyone other than Black King. I could not be in love with two men, while fighting through a divorce with a bitter jealous man.

"Bitch! This man is tryna make me his girlfriend. I did not sign up for this shit. With that horrible ass dick. FUCK!! He's so dope though. LOLOL"

"Bitch, I'm not gonna lie. I like him and I'm not even dating him. You smile so much when he's around. I love how gentle he is when he kisses you. It's so cute!"

"Ew, Bitch. I don't want to be cute. It's Hot Girl season!"

"Tinder War?"

"Duh! Let's see who's swimming in the dating pool today!"

Swipe RIGHT!

LORD knows his name would not have been my first choice and there's no way I would have ever introduced him as my man, but Tinder and high-quality gin had me seeing star material! Deyvonmetriavious. I don't know why Black folks have to be so damn different. Like, these names aren't necessary. You want to be different and unique? Start using traditional African names. Stop combining sounds that you think would sound good as you were clapping each syllable, while yelling at them, and adding, "ious" to the end! Stop! Then, we have to nerve to get mad talking about, "If you can pronounce, "Tchaikovsky', you can pronounce my baby name"! No ma'am! We have had how many thousands of years practicing his name? You just made up "Deyvonmetriavious" six months after finding out your pregnant, and we just supposed to automatically be name experts? In America? Americans don't even have a proper handle on the English language and you are expecting these names to just roll off everyone's tongue.

No.

Stop.

For real.

He was young and absolutely adorable! I have never been a fan of redbone men. I love my skin tone. I promise I do. I have grown to love my ethnically ambiguous flesh. But the idea of my high yellow skin rubbing up against someone of the same hue just makes me think of under cooked roasted chickens dancing skin to skin. I enjoy contrast, but seriously, his photos had me wanting to wiggle my southern lips across his high cheekbones. He lived in Mississippi, but he was only three hours away and willing to make the drive. We set something up for the weekend, once my children were gone. We had such great conversation the few days prior to his arrival. He had so much to say and seemed rather interesting. I asked him what his favor cuisine was, offering to cook for him. His response was Chinese. After all the Chinese meals I have sat through or cooked over the years with the Captain? Say less, Sir. I got this one.

He showed me what he was working with before coming. I thought to myself that his dick was massive and only semi hard. I wasn't prepared for what this young man was about to do to my pelvis. There's no way, I couldn't have known. He should have taken photos from different angles and sent those. I really feel like I was catfished all around. So much was different meeting in person. It just didn't make sense to me! How could this be the same person, but not all at once? Was I intoxicated when he arrived? Yes. Fucking duh. However, I was sober enough to make a traditional Taiwanese braised pork, Chinese greens, fungus, and steamed rice. Barely sober enough, but food was amazing per the usual.

As soon as he walked through the door, he threw his stuff down and started grabbing at me like a toddler grabbing for a snack. "Oh wow. I didn't think you would be this pretty in person." I had never felt pretty my entire life. It sometimes, became uncomfortable how fawned over I was by all these men. I didn't know how to find beauty in being natural and here comes man after man, banging down my door because they loved how naturally beautiful, I was. I shooed his hands away as I walked to the kitchen to make another drink. I could feel my anxiety rising. He walked behind me.

"It smells amazing and you're sexy. This is exciting! Can I see what the food looks like?" I open the pots. He pulls his head back in utter confusion. "I've never seen Asian food like that."

"What?? You've never seen real Asian food? What were you expecting? Sweet and sour pork served with hard fried rice and lo mien noodles dripping in 8-day old canola oil?"

"I mean, yeah..."

As I began to lose all interest in this imbecilic human, he creeps his hands under my hot pink mini dress. "I needed to see if your pussy was as juicy as I thought it would be. Can I get a few back shots while you cook?"

I nodded yes, as he stroked my clit. He pulled out a condom from his back pocket, pulled his pants down, and slid in between my thighs, bending me over the counter. I don't know what happened, but minutes later, I was shooting cum like a broken fire hydrant. I don't know what the fuck or how the fuck he was, but mother of God, he was. I had never cum that fast like that. He was just as shocked as I was. "I can't wait to get comfortable and fuck you right."

Bitch, when I tell you, I was thinking the same thing at that moment! I needed more of those orgasms. He was only going to be with me until the next afternoon. I have to make this count. I may have to keep him here longer. Should I just tell him to move in now and he's now a stepdaddy? Like, I don't know how to proceed with this.

Those were all valid questions in my mind, after that one lovely orgasm and less than five minutes of penetration. Shit escalated right after dinner. We ate. Good meal. He was still confused. We both drank. He wasn't at that pandemic alcoholic stage I was moving into, but he had a few to seem like he was keeping up. I rolled a few blunts, and the sun had been resting for hours. We moved to my bedroom where we planned on staying the rest of the night. I worked my way to my birthday suit and laid on my back. I was so drunk, the idea of being daddy's little rodeo rider, wasn't in the cards.

This is where I begin to feel catfished! His skin looked so moisturized in his photos. Why does his epidermis feel like he's been living in the desert plains of NeverEverLand?? He brought that backpack and didn't carry any type of cream? He didn't have lotion type skin. He had trailblazing saddle ranch skin. It didn't make no fucking sense how one person could be so fucking ashy! How are you ashy in the dark? How!? I'm so confused rubbing on this man and this man rubbing on me, but all I can think about is that thing his dick did in order to make me cum the way it did, and like a heroin addict, I was chasing my first high. I lit another blunt and smoked it while he gave me average head. Half way through the blunt, he hovers over me and slaps his dick on my thigh.

SIR!

EXCUSE ME, SIR?

You dropped a firearm on my knee. Why did you bring a gun to my...Oooh Jesus! That's that man's dick! Oh, my GAWD. What have I gotten myself into? His dick didn't feel like that standing up from the back. Why was it so heavy. What kind of grain free, fat free diet was his dick on, that made it feel like it was nothing but solid muscle? Why was it so heavy, that it hung down completely erect? I said I loved a big dick and a smile, but this ain't funny. SAFE WORD!! SAFE WORD!!! I'm drunk and high though, so all I can say is, "Safety first!" What the fuck was I thinking? He said, "Absolutely" and pulled out a condom. The alcohol starts telling me to man up! Gin is yelling at me, "Your ancestors went through what, and you're gonna sit there and act like to can't take a little heavy dick? Get a grip, Tracey!"

I listened to my ancestors. They had never pointed me down the wrong path before. I knew, just knew, this was going to end on a positive note.

Anticipation grew as he wiggled the condom on. I was pumping myself up in my head, 'You can do this! You a fucking boss BITCH! Ain't nobody got shit on you girl! These mutha fuckas don't KNOW! You gone take all that dick. You on some porn star shit!" Gin and ego showed up to the party and quickly left. Deyvonmetriavious, guided that big hunk of meat inside slowly into my tight hole with his hand. "Fuck, you pussy tight tight."

I mean, maybe. But also, you just may have a dinosaur penis and my pussy, though small, doesn't stand a chance. I was being stretched to the max, but enjoying each inch he slowly pushed into me. Then, it felt like a rock had fell into the bottom of my vagina walls. This, is where it stopped being fun. This is where everything went south. That big ass horse hung, original African, lost in time and space slave from 1834, before genes were mutated from colonization penis is rubbing upon my rectum??!! What is going on?? He is in my vagina and he is somehow fucking my anus at the same time without even being in my anus? I'm going to shit on myself. He is going to make me shit this whole entire bed!

I'm scared at this point. There is sheer terror in my spirit. My ancestors are in the back of the room whispering, "Sis, we dropped the ball on this one. We sorry. We didn't get the right photos. He should have taken them from different angles." I could not believe what was happening. I tell no lies, I was afraid. I was almost 40! I can't be shitting beds! I can't start off being a cougar like this! This is NOT the way. I can't go out like this. I turned into Rocking- Horse Rhonda real fast! "Let me ride that big dick."

I was wobbling. I didn't care. I promise I wasn't going to stay on my back a moment longer. I wiggled down his pole and channeled my inner "strong knees" and pushed through the most unexpected unnecessarily long sex one could ever experience. He wanted to have sex again the next morning; in the morning light. This man's skin had my bed looking like a winter wonderland in spring...I turned over from the back, trying to chase that high one more time. That is a drug I will never try again. He consistently contacted for well over a year after those days together. He was never allowed to my house again. I kept conversation to a minimum. I have absolutely nothing to prove in my life from that moment.

My booty still hurts, thinking about Deyvonmetriavious.

I put back man after man like liquor, in a tiny glass, at a bar in Mexico. I couldn't stop the men or the drinks...

Eight

Now, It's Time for A Breakdown

I was so bubbly and full of optimism for my future before I met him. I was finally looking at me. When I met him though? All I could see is him. All of my emotions were tied up in him. Generational trauma was tied up in how I looked at him. Seeing my mother go through man after man became tied up in how I looked at him. Seeing my father knock back women like they were nothing was now tied up in how I saw my Black King. He stole my light. I allowed him in and he stole my joy. Like a king battling for land, he defeated me and claimed my body and mind for his own. I was weak. My soul was a puddle of humility shifting frantically on the ground, needing him to contain the mess I had become. I'm losing this battle of sanity. I'm triggered beyond belief. Where is the protection you promised me? Where is the pathway for my success? You said you were a leader, but look where you have led me! I need you.

I need you.

I can't do this without you.

I have never been here.

I'm lonely.

I'm drowning.

I AM DARK NOW.

Not being able to be on the road and sell at markets during the pandemic left me financially shattered in one of the poorest states in the nation. I lost 75% of my income. I was happy that we were on lockdown because, Lord knows, I couldn't afford the gas to go anywhere. I had no choice, but to go to Captain Patriarchy for money.

"Hey there!

Our daughter's car seat has expired and I cannot afford to buy a new one right now. Will you share the car seat you have? Will you give me money, so I can buy one while she is riding with me? Will you go buy one, so you don't think I'm wasting money, and provide one for her?" I hated being at that point. I never wanted to ask him for anything. I knew my reality however. I knew that I never worked after having children because it cost more in childcare and gas to work, than to stay at home. I didn't have consistent income rolling in, and the father of my children made six figures. He could afford to buy a car seat or five.

He responded: Hello Tracey,

How long have you known our daughter's car seat was expired? You only had the kids one week last month. That means you should have extra child support money left over. Use that to buy our daughter a car seat in your car."

My children didn't matter to him. The man that was once my Captain, that I would follow blindly, was nothing but rage and revenge towards me. I used my electric bill money to buy my daughter a car seat that month. That's when bills started piling up. I cried and drank. Flashes of struggling through childhood flooded my brain. I began crying the same tears my grandmother would cry at night when she thought I was asleep. Pure agony dug its claws into my spine and pinned me to the ground. I wanted all of this to stop. It was a tsunami of emotional pain. I didn't know how to cope. There was nothing left inside me. I was lost in a mental space of trauma I had never dealt with. I was trapped with depression, anxiety, alcohol, and high-quality weed.

"I fucking hate him! Everything I gave up for his career and I have to suffer because he wants to throw little man tantrums!"

"I'm sorry."

"I was everything for that man. He couldn't stop being an arrogant dickhead!"

"I'm sorry."

"He wants to ruin my life because of that bitter ass woman he's with."

"How do you know he is still with that woman?"

"Because he doesn't know how to be alone. He's never been alone. I saw her. He's as good as she will get. They deserve each other."

"Then, why you mad?"

"I'm not mad at them being together. I told him go get a girlfriend, so he could leave me the fuck alone. It just so happened he stayed with the woman that found out her man was still fucking his wife, because his wife forced him to be honest with her. Like, and my Instagram fan? It's all so messy and weird. They are just both less than average people bitter over a woman he was never good enough for, and she will never be good enough to be. None of this has anything to do with me, however. Those are their feelings and emotions to work through."

"I just sent you money. I don't need it back. I just need to know you and the kids are taken care of. That's all that matters. You need me to come over and hold you, while we smoke and watch TV?"

"I always want you around. Come over ten minutes ago."

I cried until That Tinder Guy told me he was around the corner. I wiped tears from my eyes to pretend everything was ok.

"How long were you crying?" He asked me as he walked through my doorway.

"What?"

"Stop. How long?"

"Not long."

"Come lay on me, Pooters."

"Don't talk to me like that. Gross."

Safety. He was so safe. I stumbled and fell into him. I had no guard up with him. I could be weird and strange and bubbly and goofy; soft. I could be soft. I could be vulnerable with a man. I knew he would never hurt me. To look to his eyes and feel his care for me. It felt gently magical at times. For the first time, it wasn't about sex. I wasn't about sex. I wanted the sex to be better, but if it wasn't, it didn't matter with him.

Frat Boy Slim would call in the late hours of the night. That Tinder Guy would hold me in his arms as we laid in my bed, completely unbothered by any man trying to approach what he clearly claimed for himself. I missed the life uplifting sex Frat Boy Slim provided however.

"Bitch, what the fuck am I supposed to do?"

"Girl…Bitch…If you don't get your shit together! Do them both! You have zero commitment to neither one of those mutha fuckas. Fuck them."

I was alone. I was very drunk. It was 3:17am. Aunt Patty was hot, steamy, and needed to be stretched sideways.

"I want you. I need your dick pushing my stomach into my spine."

Fifteen minutes later, Frat Boy Slim was walking into my bedroom. I left the front door unlocked for him. My door would always be unlocked for him.

"Shit. I've been waiting for this pussy. She gets so wet and hot. Fuck, I can't wait to stick my dick inside you. Lay back so I can taste your pussy on my tongue."

I never understood how he could be so young and so smooth, yet here we were once again. I was looking down at his dick shifting my internal organs around under the flesh of my stomach. He held my legs wide open to make sure he could shove that big dick deep in my pussy. I took it all. Every inch made my pussy splash everywhere. He looked like he was attacked by water balloons and he didn't care one bit. He pushed harder into me with every orgasm I had.

"OMG, OMG, OMG, OMG, OMG, OMG...I love fucking you. You have some of the best dick God has ever created. I can't take it. It's so deep. Look at you in my stomach! Fuck! You killing my pussy."

One of those moments when I spoke like a porn star during sex and meant it. Frat Boy Slim fucked the holy spirit into my body until screaming, "LET ME LIVE IN THIS PUSSY!" Then, he nutted harder than I had seen from him and rolled over to take a nap. He deserved every ounce of sleep he got afterwards. My labias pulsed with pure euphoria. He was so incredibly good. I swear I always wanted to keep him around. He faded into dust however. He told me he felt like he was nothing more than just sex, and he wanted more time to hang out and get to know each other. "You just make me feel so comfortable. I need to be around you."

I mean, he wasn't wrong. He was nothing more than sex. Not even on a drunken cloudy day did I see a future with him. "I like the relationship we have established though. This is what it was from the beginning. I let you know upfront. No feelings were to be involved." I was sad I had to let him go, but I couldn't give him what he needed, and Captain lost his absolute mind three days later. I couldn't add any other human to manage emotionally.

I just needed some extra pants for my kids. I went to our family house to grab some. I parked in the driveway and left he kids in the car with it still running. I only needed pants, then I was getting back on the road to mail orders. I was on the phone with my grandmother trying to explain for the 900th time why I wouldn't go back to the Captain. I walked up the staircase to my children's bedroom, grabbed what I needed and as I walked down the stairs, my kids that I left in the car, were in the home, sitting on the couch watching TV.

"Where's the grill, Tracey?"

Is this silly mutha fucka for real? A BBQ grill? He thinks I'm about to fight with him in front of these kids over a BBQ grill that his small ass didn't even purchase? He has lost his entire mind. "Captain, I am not going to argue with you in front of the kids." His question was on repeat, while I worked to get my children out of the house. He followed two feet behind me asking me the same fucking question over and fucking over. I knew where he was going to take this and I wanted no parts of it.

When Captain Patriarchy gets angry, he loses sight of everything logical. He was hyper focused on a BBQ grill and he wasn't going to back down. The kids went into the hallway to put on their shoes. My son stood at the backdoor waiting to leave. My daughter sat, pouting on the bench, slowly easing her shoes on. I put my hand on her shoulder to nudge her off the bench, "Ma'am, we have to go. I have to get to the post office before it closes."

"LOOK AT YOU!! YOU'RE HURTING HER! AND, I'M THE ONE THAT'S UNSTABLE???" The Captain has left the building, folks. He is no longer with us. I don't know what dimension that man went to, but he had most definitely left reality. He snatched our four-year-old daughter up into his arms like some rogue bodyguard coming in to save the day based upon a false call. He looked like the biggest fucking moron. That was one of the many situations, where I was embarrassed to say I had children by him.

He ran into the guest bedroom in the hallway, holding our little girl like a human body shield against his chest, and attempted to slam and lock the door behind him. I chased after him. With my foot in the air, ready to kick the entire door off the fucking hinges, I see my son. My baby boy's eyes were wide open with fear and panic.

What am I doing?

Dear God...What am I doing to my son?

I was putting my children through the same bullshit I faced as a child. I vowed to never do that to them. I vowed to stick with their dad no matter what. I was so selfish for leaving. Look at the aftermath. Look what I have caused. I saw regret and pain and sorrow for all of us. I walked to my son. "I'm so sorry, Boog. You should have never seen any of this. I'm so sorry for all of this. I'm going to go outside and collect my emotions, like I teach you, ok?" I walked out of the back door and called Black King.

"This mutha fucka is crazy!! He used my daughter as body armor, Daddy!"

"Oh, I'm Daddy again?"

"I'm not doing this with you right now. I can't believe this shit! He is holding my kids hostage!!!" I conveyed the story to Black King.

"Tracey. Don't NOBODY wanna be with their kids 24/7. He's going to give those kids back at some point. Take your ass home and go play with that pretty ass pussy and send me the video."

"Don't you think you have enough videos of me?"

"Fuck no! I will never get enough of that good ass pussy. Why you think that man is so mad? He ain't never getting that pussy again, but he gotta look at kids that look and act like you all the time."

"Oh, my pussy is good to you now?"

"You know you got some good ass pussy. Got me sucking on my fingers, thinking about tasting you right now. Now, go home and let me see you rub one out."

Fuck. I loved how nasty Black King was. He could turn my frown upside down, in no time flat! As I wrapped up my conversation and walked to my car, the police rolled up. The fuck? I know this man did NOT call the police?! "Daddy, this man called the fucking police!"

An adorably cute clean shaven white male officer stepped out of his vehicle, "Hello Ma'am. I'm here because someone was pinched." He said it in such a gentle Southern accent, I thought he said, "punched".

"Who got punched??"

"No Ma'am, PINCHED." He said it with a smile and soft chuckle.

"Daddy, this fucking fool called the police and told them he got pinched! Y'all for real have to show up to calls when someone says they were pinched? Y'all take pinching seriously?"

"No, we don't take pinching seriously. They probably showed up because that shit is funny!"

I didn't find the humor in any of this. Nothing was funny to me. I put on my adult face though. "Chile, excuse me? That clown called y'all saying I pinched him?"

"Yes Ma'am. Before I go in, may I ask you a few questions? Can I ask you to get off the phone?"

"Babe, I'm going to call you back."

Forty minutes of the officer going in and out of the house talking to my ex-husband and I separately. My ex ended up with a scratch on his arm. He said it was from me. That jackass probably scratched his arm on the door trying to reenact scenes from the movie, Taken. No one told him to overreact and meltdown like he's trying out for the main role in the 2009 film Obsessed. Dear God, why did I have kids with that man? The sheer shame I held. I walked away without my children that day. They were calm watching TV. The officer felt, since they were calm, it was better to not agitate them any further. I went home and drank an entire bottle that night. I watched memories of my mother lying on a pulled-out sofa bed, barely coherent from can after can of Colt 45, and my father's eyes half rolled into his eyelids doped up, as I slipped into the darkness of my own living Hell on my living room floor. I woke up in the middle of the night with my face stuck to hardwood floors by slobber thinking about my Black King.

"How are you?"

"I'm good. How are you?"

"I miss you."

"I miss you too."

"I need to feel your body on top of mine."

"Say less. When?"

"I want to be in control."

"Say less. When?"

"I want to do some things we haven't tried before."

"Tracey, when? I am home for a few days."

"Tomorrow afternoon."

"I'm all yours."

The desire to taste his skin was beyond measure. I didn't think Black King would concede so easily. I showed up in blue lingerie; his favorite color with black 6" inch heels with a bow on top. My lips were burgundy wine in color.

"Fuck. You're so sexy. I missed this shit. I would fuck you every day if I could."

"You could, but you play with my heart too much. Take those pants off and lay down."

I crawled between his thighs and held on to his massive piece of man meat, slowly rubbing his manhood across my lips. I kissed the tip, then swallowed him whole, while looking into his eyes. "Fuckkkkkkk...Tracey." He slowly lowered his head back towards the pillow, falling into the cosmic pleasure of passion we shared. I forced his legs into a "V" and lowered my mouth downward. I stroked his dick, while my tongue whimsically danced over his testicles and inner thighs. My Black King was losing control. His body grinded the bed. His legs slowly began to shake. To see him in such ecstasy made my pussy drip. I stopped abruptly. Like, an assertive little kitten demanding affection, I crawled on top of his body towards his face. In straddling position, I rubbed the cum from my pussy with two of my fingers. I licked one finger in his face, "Look what you did to my pussy. You making me leak, Daddy." I pushed the second finger down his throat. "Taste what you do to me." I felt his heart drop towards the box spring.

I bounced back down between his legs, and began licking his asshole. Black King grabbed onto the sheets, then dug his fingernails into my back and growled something far beyond animalistic. His body tensed up in stroke position for several seconds. I began to worry. I started thinking to myself, "Did I just kill this man? OMG!! Could you imagine going to jail for fucking a cop to death!!! That is Pussy of The Year award type of shit right there! I think I might be ok with that crime. Bad Bitch Pussy."

He breathed.

I'm back to reality with him. Our bodies perfectly formed together; I take my King down into pleasure very few are afforded to experience in life. He calls my name as my tongue rolls from his rectal opening to the tip of his dick, and down his shaft. Almost an hour later, he asks for a moment to breathe. I pull back with a devil's grin on my face. He smiles back accordingly. "Really, Tracey?"

"Yes. Really. I have wanted to do that to you for so very long. Your ass is amazing."

"I'm about to show you what amazing is."

I slightly tilt my head back getting ready to give him a cute little pose, but I didn't have time. As I sat onto of my feet while on my knees, at the foot of his bed, he pounced towards me. He launched his arm from his body and grabbed me by my throat, forcing my tiny body backwards. I stopped breathing from the anticipation. Looking into my core, he said in a voice from our past lives, "Rotate your body to face the ground."

My body was shaking something not of this Earth. We were not in our bodies any longer. I obediently followed my King's orders and rotated my body, while my neck was still in his enormous right palm. He let go and grabbed onto both of my hips, pulling my ass high in the air. "Don't you fucking move."

"I would never."

"Shut the fuck up. You gone know when to talk and when not to."

"Yes, Sir."

Face down, ass up, he leans forward pushing his African lineage penis into my womb lobby as far as I can take it, and pulls my head back towards his face by my neck at the same time. I let out a scream only the spirit world could hear. In the shape of a yoga pose, he pumped that fat Black dick into my rib cage, "Look what you did to my dick. You feel how hard this shit is? That's why you my fucking Bitch. I fucking love you."

"I love you too, Daddy."

"I know Daddy's little Bitch does. You take this dick so good."

"I love taking it for you. I want it all. Don't stop. Make me nut all over your dick."

"Fuck yes! Squirt on my dick. Ahhhhhh, you pussy is so good."

Hours of sweating through the Alabama summer heat with no air conditioning, we went back and forth between worlds and past lives. It was nothing but him and I for hours. "Get on your knees and play with those big ass tits. I want to nut in your mouth."

"As you wish."

I turned upright, opened my mouth and stuck out my tongue like a dog waiting for a treat from its master. "Fuuuuuuuuuucccckkkkkkkkk." Hot cum trickled down my throat. I swallowed every drop of him. I refused to waste even a small droplet. I continued to suck until he was dry. We sat down on the bed next to each other cracking jokes and talking about how amazing our sex is. I wanted to stay in his world forever. I needed it. I began thinking about being held by That Tinder Guy.

I stood up to put my clothes on.

"You going?"

"Yes. You know you don't fucking want me here. You just missed this pussy."

"I do want you here. I do need to be alone right now though."

"Even more reason, it's best if I leave now. We aren't fighting. We feel amazing. Let's leave it at that."

Before I walked out the door, he swooped me off my feet by my lower back, and pulled me towards his lips. He kissed me with the only love he knew how to give me. I let him melt onto me as long as he craved, then corrected my posture and emotions, and walked to my car to text That Tinder Guy.

"Hey, what are you doing? I really wanna cuddle with you and watch movies."

"I think you love me, Tracey."

"Gross. Come over, Weirdo."

That Tinder Guy was right. I did love him. I loved him in the most organic way. I went home to wash my King off of me and lay in the lap of That Tinder Guy's comfort and ease. I dove down a hole of confusion. How did I get here? What brought me to this point? I'm breaking.

Nine

Babylon

Running away from one man, poorly trying to escape a second, running to a third, reluctantly letting go of a fourth, sprinkled with cautionary dick. I was creating an empire of dick, but the foundation was toxic as fuck. It constantly shifted with each new dick I tried to lay. I was losing control of myself. I was falling away from everything. There was no one there to catch me. Ashley Madison was falling faster than I was, grabbing up for me to catch her; I was blind. We were so blind. Every time we reached for the hand of one another, we somehow managed to push each other farther and farther into a spiral of morbidly hysterical depression.

"Girl, I was telling him about all the other cops I was talking to. He was asking me questions like I didn't know he was trying to find out if I was fucking them or not. HAHAHA"

"lmfaooooooo.

Does he know any of them? Wait... did you tell him about all of them?"

"YES! HAHAHAHAHAHA Girl, I'm over here in TEARS!!! He said Pootie Pie has a white woman baby mama. He didn't marry her. He said she was pretty and they have BEAUTIFUL children. He didn't understand why he would be out cheating? Hahaha And, he said that Big and Timid wouldn't have hit it right no matter how big his dick is. Bitch! Fuck no, I didn't tell him about all of them. hahahahaha"

"BITCH, HE JEALOUS!!! HAHAHAHAHAHHAAHA!!!"

"HAHAHHAHAHAHAHAAHAHAAHHAHAHAA *LAUGHS IN DEVIL'S JOY*"

"He said he wouldn't have been mad if I fucked them because I'm still his. Girl, he's delusional. He said I'm just like his mom."

He was right. I was his. That Tinder Guy offered pure unconditional love. He valued all that I was. I was myself when I was with him, yet I couldn't give him what he deserved because I was loyal to my Black King. I gave my body freely laying with man after man. With each stroke from someone other than my Black King, pushed life from skin. Darkness was my light. I saw no reprieve. Rock bottom called to me. I couldn't hear at first. I didn't ignore her calling me. With every whisper I tip toed closer and closer, not knowing I was being pushed off the ledge. "What did you say? I can't hear you. I need to come closer for absolutely no fucking reason."

"We were lying in bed and he was telling me about all the silly cops that cheat on their wives. Ain't nobody loyal in the South. That Southern Hospitality is to cover up their indiscretions. lol"

"Bitch! I can't! He snitching on everyone to make sure you know he is top dog. It's cute and pathetic at the same time. I'm here for it. ahahahahaaha He really fucking loves you."

"Bitch, he told me! He was looking me in my eyes, kissing me talking about, 'I love you, Tracey.' He was on some intimate love-making shit after that ungodly sex we had a few weeks ago, BITCH!! hahahahahahaha He held me so tight all night long. There's just something about being around that man. Just to be in his arms...oooh Chile..."

"I wish someone would tell me they loved me. You are so lucky. I'm happy for you."

Ashley wanted the sensation of being fawned over as I was. She was dicked down like no other, but not even her constant would give her love. She deserved it, but she refused to work for it. It continuously slipped from her grasp with every dick she put her lips upon. Her admiration for me obtaining some type of love, began being overshadowed by a strange unspoken obsession. I had no one but Ashley. I couldn't be alone. I ignored the signs and went skipping hand in hand down Destruction Lane. We were off to pick up more dicks to lay on our foundation.

"He hasn't said we are committed though, so until then, wanna play Tinder War? Who ain't got the Rona, and got good dick?!"

"BITCH! HAHAHAHAHAAHA Swipe RIGHT!!! hahahahaha"

Team Tracey would like to welcome, Entanglement.

"Bitch, he fine fine, huh? I like him. I'mma bust all over his eyeballs! I'mma burn my love into his young little soul. LMAO!"

"BITCH!!???? What the fuck did you just say????????" She sent 30 laughing face emojis after. She sent 4 laughing gifs.

"I said what I said."

Black King was never going to commit to me. He just didn't want to let go of my pussy. He acted like he knew me so well, yet subtly manipulated me into a wreck of a woman, completely insecure and doubtful of every move I made. Nothing was right. Everything was wrong. Laying in my pussy was the only thing that was right. All this energy could have been spent upon growing my company. I could have worked on repairing myself. I was working on taking on spiritual baggage, fucking men that didn't even deserve an innocent glance at my mons pubis behind the fabric of panties.

The emptiness and displaced emotions those men felt was being humped into my peace. I was filled with chaos, distorting my reality with dick and liquor. Sip. Lick. Suck. Fuck. Rinse. Repeat.

Crown of my head down, I was in a free fall.

Deeper.

Deeper.

I continue to fall and you still won't catch me. You said you would be there and you are not present.

This putrid smell of dishonor strangles my neck.

Deeper.

Deeper.

I'm foaming at the mouth for your validation. I need you to tell me I'm safe. TELL ME!

Deeper.

Deeper.

I have beat you down for the last time.

I have called you out of your name for the last time.

Your love is gone because I was not capable of loving someone more than my baggage.

How many times do I have to say sorry before you come back to me?

Anxiety had me 1943 helpless white womaning all over my house. I continued to think the worst of something that was attempting to get back on track. Why was I out searching for more bullshit to add to an overflowing plate?

TIME OUT!!

There were way too many players on the field. I was losing track of my men. I was sending photos of Markontrious to This Clown, trying to play it off like I'm making fun of other men. If a man wants your pussy bad enough, he will believe absolutely anything you say to him. I started telling the same idiotic lies to men, that men would allow to freely roll off their tongue when speaking to me. I screamed, "TIME OUT" but nothing stopped. Time went faster and faster. I became a manic ball of sexual insanity.

I filled the pain of that acknowledgement with the youngest member of Team Tracey. He was my Entanglement. To the windows, to the walls, I made sweat drip down his balls! Praise to the Lort! Yes, I did. If fucking him was wrong, there were times I didn't want to be right. Other times? I was sober. I knew anything under 26 was going to end poorly. In my heart of hearts, I knew. Let the church say "Amen". But, on that day of the year of our Lord and Savior, Jesus Christ, 2020, I threw caution to the wind and laughed! He was so got damn adorable. AGGGHHH!! If I was a teenager, and he was in a boy band, he would have been like,

Justin Timberlake or Joey McIntyre. Well, in photos from the waist up. Full body photos would have been like, Joey Fatone. Like, he's still cute, but even at a young age, you know genetics are not going to be kind to his lower half.

23 years a young man, looking well-groomed and dapper. Clearly, an older woman had her paws on this strapping young lad prior to me. I don't blame her one little bit. Come here you tasty well-built, dark-toned melanin drop. Making me do the Winnie the Pooh, honey shake.

"Girl, I tried talking to him. He's so boring. He will only type like two or three words." Every once and a while, I had to double check my swipe rights with Aunt Sug. If she fucked them, I wasn't touching them. I will never be that desperate for dick, and let me tell you! I have done some desperate shit... whew...

I was shocked! He was writing me paragraphs in my Tinder DM's. It was like she and I were talking about two different people. He wanted to stay up all night and stare at each other via FaceTime like love sick school kids via video chat. Yuck. Where was this boring guy she was talking about?

"I finally remember where I know you."

"What do you mean? We met on here, Silly. Are you about to tell me you've been stalking me for the past three years, and Tinder finally gave you an alibi? Am I about to end up missing on the news? I am, huh? I knew I should have logged off Tinder a LONG time ago... fuck..."

"What the fuck? LMAOOOOO!!! No! You good. For real. I used to work at the back hand coffee shop before the shutdown. I saw you there. I will never forget your face. You said something slick, then walked away. I wanted to follow you. I couldn't though. The woman behind you told me to go follow you. You had me thinking about walking off my job!"

"Oh my gosh! That's so funny. That sounds like something I would do. I'm known to have a rather sharp tongue. I'm sure it's why I stand out in the South. And, the strange fetish y'all have for red bone women. Dip her in a pot of the ancestors voodoo oils, and y'all will chase us to the ends of the Earth. I have no clue why."

"Lmaooooo!!! You one of those Erykah Badu women, huh?"

"You gone let me touch that dick, so you can find out?"

"Oh Shit!"

"That didn't answer my question, now did it?"

"Omg! I was hoping to get a chance to run into you again one day to ask you on a date. Look at God."

"Lmaooo! Does that mean, you're going to bring me some hard dick and blow my back out?"

"Say less. What's the address?"

He had no clue what he was about to get himself into. And, I will admit, I didn't know either. When they want me badly, they always want to be passionate with me. They bumble along my body, dripping spit into my mouth, trying to rub their tongue against mine. A guy I kissed in high school hit me up on social media, telling me how sexy I was and when I was ready for some real pipe, I could give him a call. Sir, if the kiss is any indication of the dick, you can lay that "real pipe" in someone else's yard. You ain't finna be leaking slobber into my mouth like a teething infant. No, Sir. I do not want any of that!

That's the way I felt about my Entanglement once he pressed his lips against mine for the first time. He pulled back, holding my face with his hand, staring in my eyes. I thought, Oh no... this shit.

"I can't believe you almost had me killed!" He threw his head back and laughed.

"Look, I gave you the right directions. You read them incorrectly. That's not my fault. My neighbor has guns and gardening tools. You will fuck around and find out showing up in her yard and she doesn't know you!" Ms. Pauline from around the corner was no joke! Entanglement ended up walking into her backyard garden, thinking it was my garden backyard. Ms. Pauline came sneaking around the side of her house about to stab him, as he screamed, "I'm looking for Tracey!!" She put the sheers down, and guided him to my house where he was now working to remove my clothing.

And, hocking mucus bubbles into my cheeks.

I'm pouting, by the way.

"I have dreamed about eating your pussy. I'm so ready for this."

Dear Jesus,

Why for art thou bringeth me this young stallion to break?

Sincerely,

I'm Going to Fuck This Boy's World Up

I jumped back on that bed like a kid jumping into a ball pit! Let's ride my dude!! I'm ready too!!! I didn't know I was ready until now, but your enthusiasm has my juices following! You have got my club jumping!

My coffee is grinding, if you will. Give me all that sweet lickity split my labias!

Whomever the cougar was that got to that little boy first? Ma'am, job well done! I mean, you are a professional hoe and your guidance and quality of work shows. I hope you know this wherever you are in this country. The thing he does to your asshole with his finger and his tongue? Chef's kiss, Bitch. You out did yourself with that pupil.

My entanglement showed me how much he dreamed of me. I have to admit, it kind of turned me on and reminded me of how much Mr. Inconsistent enjoyed fucking me. With my ass in the air and his thumb palm deep in my asshole, I hear a snap, and he slides his dick into me. The whole congregation just said, "Amen" all together.

SIS! YOU DID SUCH A GOOD JOB WITH THIS MAN!

Three strokes in and I sent this man down Splash Mountain! "OH MY FUCKING GOD! LOOK WHAT YOU JUST DID TO MY PUSSY! MMMmmmmmmmm..." My body was shaking. There was human liquid puddling at his feet. The tone in my voice went lower as I worked to control my breathing. I looked back into his eyes, "Fuck me harder. How many times can you make me squirt before you nut?" He didn't want to stop. He began pumping into my body with force, sounding like someone sucking gravy off a plate. He began screaming as he slipped in the puddle at his feet and fell deeper into my hole.

"This is the best pussy ever!" He yelled right before letting out a scream of panic to rip off the condom before nutting onto my ass cheeks. I couldn't believe what just happened. That was fucking incredibly good! I was so sad about losing Frat Boy Slim. Entanglement seemed to be the next best thing. I fell forward onto my stomach and laid there a bit. I was taking the in exhilaration of it all. I was actually going to save this young man's real name into my phone! If he wants a to-go sack lunch, I'm going to make it for him. He can even have an extra juicebox! He earned it! As I rolled over to take a total glance at his body, my elbow gave out and I fell back down onto the bed. He asked, "Are you ok?" I told him yes and what happened, but honestly, I fell out of shock!

How dare this young man show up to my house and do all these amazing things to me then, have the impudence to, freely, walk around my bed room carrying somebody's grandma's booty! NO! I don't want this! I was about to make a life for him as my new side dude, and he pulls a stunt like this!? Like, THIS? I packed up the joy I had and put it in a coffin to get ready to bury. When I tell you, the thrill was gone? Thrill had sent me divorce papers. Speaking of which; I was getting tired of asking for.

I heard nothing Grandma Shirlene, I mean, Entanglement was saying. He needed to leave my house. I was about to drink myself into a coma. As he shook them big cheeks into the bathroom to clean himself off, I was checking texts and emails. I didn't have a problem with the texts that were coming in. Ashley was sending some pretty killer gifs, asking me what the dick was like. I typed back, "That grandma can lay some pipe!" Then, I checked my emails and found myself all the way fucked up.

"Tracey,

The kids well being (mental, emotional, physical, and safety) is all I care about. Whatever you and I have is completely separated. That being said, one night this week I overheard you telling the kids about your cop friend, I asked them if they know that friend and Osumare said yes, he's Leonard. At the same time Xolani freaks out and tells Osumare to not say anything and he looked extremely scared like they just did something wrong. I reassured him that it's fine and he's not in trouble, however he looks so disturbed/scared and started to tear up. I do not know what you told the kids, but the fact that he seems to fear for answering a question is not ok with me. I don't care about your business, what I do care is my children's well-being. If they are with someone or around someone new, they shouldn't be afraid to talk to their dad about it. It is important that we both know who the kids are with and hanging around. It bothered me very much that Xolani seemed that scared. I need to know that my children has no worries to tell me or you anything, free and with no consequences or judgement, especially when it comes to them being around new people. If the kids meet a new friend of mine, I have no problem with them telling you. If you don't want the kids to share your business with me maybe you should be more aware of what you tell as share with them. They are kids and they need to have no fear talking to their parents about.

What ER/hospital did you go to? Did you get any test results back? You have posted you have Covid and Zinc poisoning, however when I ask you for your test results you say you can't get them. So how is it that you know you have covid and zinc poisoning. Both are serious matter and if you don't have proof of having both or the you are truly better and cleared by a medical physician, how would I know our children will be safe staying with you? Did you have fever or symptoms last week before I dropped them off? If you did, you failed to mentioned it to me. If you would of told me you've been running a fever and cannot take care of the kids, I wouldn't have dropped them off. You not telling your health condition does not help anyone especially the kids. If you don't think it is best practice to make sure your actually fine before coming to get the kids, I cannot trust you with the kids. And you coming over here please do not with proof you're well from the doctors. I am not going to allow you to risk the kids health because of your lack of better judgement in these pandemic times.

Aside from that, I am not stupid as you think I am, you should really stop being such a hypocrite. You give me so many rules and you know what I've been very good about it to make sure you don't freak out, but apparently those rules is only set for me and not you. That is not how being cordial works, again I've been nothing but accommodating to you since your moved out mid January. Know that your cop "friend" which you also call your "boyfriend" is public news. And sounds like he has met the kids or that the kids know him. Strange how it's not ok for me for me to even introduce a new friend to the kids but it's ok when you do it. And going back to the well-being of the children, if your cop "friend" is still on duty and hanging out with you, that's risking the kids health as he's exposed to the public on a consistent basis. It is also very strange you continue to say how dare I called the cops on you and how they could of killed you. I was very clear on what I was going to do and clearly and repeatedly asked you not to come over and if you did I had to call the cops. That was exactly what happened. Not a surprise to you. So again one day a cop will kill you but next you're ok dating one, also you have taught the kids to fear cops, remember when you got pulled over on one of your many times, this one stood out to me because you told me when the cops pulled you over the kids asked the cops if he was going to kill them. I understand very well what is going on in our world and especially these time it worries me what your telling our children and what type of example your setting for them. From fearing cops one day, to hey here's a good friend cop, to whatever you told the kids to not tell me and Xolani freaking out and almost crying. Think of his mental health, is this good for him? To fear telling his dad the truth?

I am not trying keep the kids away from you but due to the nature of COVID-19, it is imperative that you and I have a clear picture of what the kids are potentially being exposed to. Not knowing your true diagnosis of your health would be a risk to the kids. Taking the kids to the store is a necessity, I take all precautions going into the store, leaving and when we get home. They have face mask on while in the store and I keep them close where they are not grabbing at things or going close to people. I avoid isles which have too many people and return later so they are not exposed. And all this is done to minimize their exposure and time being next to strangers. You want to take them a an event, while you're working. How are you able to watch the kids and do the event, both you and I know they love running around and talking to people. Do you really think it's a wise decision to do that? As you said before about your 14days quarantine, it hasn't been 14 days and so I am not sure how serious you take this pandemic. After 14 days, the kids can go with you, but you still need to provide paperwork showing you have passed clean bill of health."

Did this man just send me a copy and pasted rant via email? I was at my wits end with Captain Patriarchy. How did he have the time to have a girlfriend with a child and stalk me with insane allegations? I texted him that I was not ok days prior; I needed help, and that balding bitch took the kids and left me for dead. I should not have had one of the best orgasms known to womankind, then roll over to Grandma Jackson, only to roll back over and read that shit from a broken, broken man. I told Entanglement that I had some work emails to take care of and we had to cut things short. He left with his shoulders down. I did walk him to the door and kissed him goodbye though. On a drunk night in the dark, I won't even know what he looks like from the back. *"You're fishing for information into my personal life, which I do not have to explain to you. The kids have not been around anyone you do not know and/or have met, so no. No, I am not a hypocrite. Tomorrow is the end of my 14 day quarantine. I have two meetings in the afternoon. I'll be there afterwards. If you don't care to be around me, please make arrangements to stay elsewhere. I will be staying in our home for a few days. It's been over 2.5 months now. Please provide me with the amendments to the divorce agreement."*

I responded back as calmly as I could, but I was thinking, "Mary Elizabeth! If you don't get your crazy stalking ass off of the internets and out of my emails! What the entire fuck is wrong with you? I thought you were still seeing your therapist?" Hearing my grandma complain about the drug addict shit my dad would do, flashed in my head. Listening to the wind whisper how much my uncle loved touching me as a little girl knocked me into my kitchen looking for anything that would drown out my nightmares. I didn't gain weight that summer. I was dehydrated from crying, cumming, and finding new ways to make an adult beverage in fancy vintage glassware. My tears were made of high-end alcohol.

I wanted so badly to be happy and healthy after divorce. I wanted to find love and serenity. My life had become the equivalent to a telenovela on fentanyl, living in Miami, Florida, working part time washing windshields at a 7Eleven. Every emotion of every poor decision laid the infectious mortar of my Babylon walls of dick. I walked around my Fortress of Despair naked and insecure behind the walls. To be worth so much and feel so little. Everywhere I began to walk, the ground made of sharp glass sliced the bottoms of my fragile feet. Any type of joy slowly bled from my body. I couldn't take much more. Babylon was falling.

"What are you doing?"

"I was about to call you and see if you wanted to smoke."

"I do. Come through."

I quickly changed the sheets from the night before. An entire day passed me by and I was so intoxicated, I didn't realize I drank myself asleep for almost 20 hours. I brushed my teeth, washed my ass, and smiled brightly. That Tinder Guy walked into my house and began kissing me. "I want to put my dick in you so bad." I fell to my knees and began sucking him hard. I promise, you won't walk into my house talking like that and I won't do something about it! I sucked him to his liking, then stood up and guided him to my bedroom. I bent over to grab a condom from the bottom drawer of my nightstand. That Tinder Guy grabbed my hips and slid his raw dick inside me. He felt so good. I got caught up in the moment. I let him slide back and forth a few more times before stopping him. He nutted as soon as he pulled out the last time. We didn't even get to use the condom. Black King was the only man to have me raw other than my husband and Chicago Dick. I was feeling a bit betrayed by That Tinder Guy. I didn't tell him he could do that. I wasn't ready for that with him. He sat down on my bed with his pants at his ankles, "I think I love you."

"This pussy took you out today, huh?" I tried to act like I didn't hear what he just said. That was left for only my King. What was he doing?

"Who else are you fucking, Tracey?" My ex-husband was screaming at me through phone calls and voicemails, and endless texts, and we can't forget to mention emails.

"Yes, I love you too, Tracey." My Black King was bowing to his queen.

"Hey...what are you up to?" Frat Boy Slim was missing me.

"I'm not going to lie; you have me turned around. I can't stop thinking about you. I want to be with you again." That's how Entanglement is going to speak to me? Proper communication and grammar? He continued to text me how he wanted to be on top of me, while looking into my eyes. What is up with my eyes? Are they some kind of crystal balls that allow men to see a different kind of love? Do they not know it will fade when they get to know me? I'm going to find some way to fuck it up. I'm too wounded to fight for love. I don't give a fuck one got damn bit. Just fuck me and leave me alone!

"Good morning beautiful", seven men would text with no punctuation.

"Hey Sexy", would be sent with eyeball emojis by four men.

Dick pic after dick pic being sent via social media like it was September and children were starting to mail in the Christmas wish lists to Santa! My Pussy is not sliding down your winter pole! Leave me alone!!!! My heart was missing. My mind was on overload. My walls caught on fire and burning to the ground all around me. Like a possessed voodoo high-priestess, I walked through the flames and destruction unbothered to the naked eye. I held my head with the Devil's pride.

"Hey... I have to tell you something. I came inside you a little bit yesterday."

"FUCKING WHAT?"

"Yeah..I didn't think I was going to nut that quick feeling you raw for the first time. Got damn your pussy is hot."

"What the fuck is wrong with you? I could lose everything I have been fighting for! This is everything I have earned this entire fucking marriage and you want to fuck around and nut in me a little bit!? I can't fucking believe you!?"

That Tinder Guy lost everything we were building in that one conversation. He took advantage of the moment fucking me raw, knowing damn good and well he was horrible with nutting quickly with me. Flashes of losing my children in the state of Alabama popped in and out of my head. Having a baby by one man, but legally it belonged to another because I'm still married in the state of Alabama.

I'm pretty sure it's illegal to have an abortion in the state of Alabama... How the FUCK did I end up in Alabama?

"Hey Bitch! Wanna do some drugs?? LOLOLOLOL"

"Bitch! What kind? Want to just do a bunch over the weekend?"

Epilogue

Whoa! Am I right? Like, how does it just end like that? Who does that? Remember 1980 sitcoms in May? Those cliff hangers? BOOM! Just hit you with a 1980's cliff hanger! How many months did all that commotion go on in her life? Do you think it's still going on? Does she do drugs, then find out she is pregnant? Does she end up with any of them?

OMG! What if, years later, it's still going on! Could you imagine? Susan!!? Rebecca!? Call Linda! Tell everyone there's going to be a sequal! We need to know what happened next? Is we or ain't we finding love and happiness and inner peace???

Go grab some tea, go to the bathroom, go take a shower, stretch, and I'll be back with part 2 before you know it!

About Author

Born and raised in Southern California, Tracey now lives in Birmingham Alabama with her two children and four dogs. She is the full time founder and sole operator of California Country Organics Body Care, (www.calibamaorganics.com). Tracey loves to garden by turning her land into walking garden space with man-made ponds she created. She ended up finding a passion for writing as she worked to mentally escape life. Tracey focuses on learning how to love herself and those around her in the most authentic way, and actively mind her business.

Acknowledgments

Erin, thank you for being the other half of my brain. Amber for loving me all these years. Aareona for being the first person to put into my head that I could call myself a writer. Danielle for offering unconditional love. Renee for seeing my voice and my power. Dagmar, you made sure I achieved.

To You, thank you for showing me what a man could feel like.

Notes

OMG!! What's going to happen next, Erin!

Made in the USA
Columbia, SC
23 July 2023